EVERY LOVE

By LK Collins

Copyright © 2015 by LK Collins

Print Edition

978-0-578-16918-7

Every Love

A novel by LK Collins

Cover Design by RE Creatives

Edited by Lisa Christman, Adept Edits

Formatting by Paul Salvette, BB eBooks

Photography by Aleksandr Petrunovskyi

DEDICATION

To my editor, Lisa, you are simply remarkable.

CHAPTER 1

-Nate-

Oh fuck! The bathroom is covered in blood. It's smeared down the wall and pooled around my mom's head, where she's lifelessly lying flat on her face. Fear freezes me. *What in the world happened?* The shower curtain is ripped down, her bloody hand print is smeared along the side of the tub where she struggled to get herself up.

"Ma," I yell, finally willing myself to move to her side. I touch her back to wake her and suddenly I'm back in Afghanistan. I push away the images assaulting me that I have worked so hard to suppress. But still, before my eyes is a wounded soldier, shot, bloody, and hanging on to life. *God dammit, stop!* This is my mom, not that place. I'm scared to move her and know better than to even try. My worst fear in this world is something happening to her. Moving my trembling hands to shake her a little more, I'm about to lose it. I don't want to hurt her, but I also want to wake her any way possible. My heart is thudding against the walls of my chest as I grab her wrist to see if she has a pulse. I sit in silence, fighting to hear her heart. *How did this happen? Did someone hurt her? Where is all this blood coming from?* My mind races, all the while I'm listening. I'm not sure if what I feel is her heart or mine, but I go with my gut and hop up the best that I can, my prosthetic making it hard to move around.

Quickly I swipe the phone off of her nightstand and grab a towel as I drop back to my knees, dialing 911. Tears stream down my face looking at her this way. The blood is coming from a gash on her head, and I try to click into numb soldier mode as I press the towel onto the wound to stem the bleeding. Someone had to have done this to her. There's simply too much blood for her to have slipped and fallen on her own. I feel the panic overtaking me, worming through the numbness.

"911, what's your emergency?"

"It's—" I choke, staring at her weak body.

"Hello? Sir, what's your emergency?"

"My…My mom…I…I don't know what…." My voice is shaky and I'm struggling through each word. "She's…she's unconscious and—"

"Is she breathing, sir?"

Fuck, there's a lot of blood. My mind flashes back to the battlefield, my chest tightens, I'm frozen.

"Sir, I need to know if she's breathing?"

"I…"

"I'm routing an ambulance to you. Are you at 211 Riverdale?"

"Uh huh."

"Sir, now please tell me, is your mom breathing?"

"She's facedown, so… I don't know."

"Is her airway clear?"

Leaning over her, I look at my mom's face and gently brush her hair out of the way. I can see that nothing is blocking her mouth or nose. Her eyes are closed and her poor glasses are smashed to hell, barely over her eyes.

"There's…" *Fuck!*

"Sir? Her airway?"

"It's clear."

"Good, does she have a pulse?"

"I think so."

I hear the dispatcher in the background speak to someone, then she comes back on the line.

"The ambulance should be there in less than a minute, just leave her 'til the medics arrive. Are you okay to get off the phone and open your front door?"

"Yeah," I say and hang up.

I take a deep breath and try to push the panic down, unlocking the door in a haze. I need to get my shit together. Running back to my mom, I rest my head softly against hers, I cry and just pray that she'll be okay. She has to be. I've already lost one woman in my life, so I sure as hell can't lose another. Lying this close to her, I can feel her breathing.

Thank God. Pulling the towel away, I check and see that her head is no longer bleeding. That's good. But again my damn mind gets the best of me and morbid thoughts take over. I envision her in a casket, my dad and I crushed with grief standing over her, and the pain of it is as real as if I was standing right there, right now.

All of a sudden the room is flooded with EMTs. "Sir, I need you to get up," one of them says, his voice so faint as I struggle to come out of the grief brought on by my vision. Where did it even come from? He gently helps me up as I'm still having a hard time processing things.

"What happened?" one of them asks me as the others begin to work on her.

I replay the story the best that I can, fighting to stay calm and in the moment. Then out of the blue – a flashback to the day Arion collapsed in the hallway outside of her condo, when I showed up like an asshole and scared the shit out of her. She had no idea that I was alive, and the pure shock alone caused her to faint.

Watching my mom just as helpless makes my world spin. Everything inside of me aches as my vision bounces between her, Arion, and war.

CHAPTER 2

The walls are white, and it smells like Germany. It's the same stench I dealt with when I was recovering there after being held hostage for close to a year. Images of my mom flood my mind, her blood sprayed everywhere, her lifeless body lying in a pool of it. The images flash from her to my fellow soldiers, and back again.

I've worked my ass off not to go back to that place and now…here I am. My body is numb and every single ounce of energy is drained from me. I put my sleeve under my nose to try and block out the scent and attempt to focus on the TV. Unfortunately, my cell phone is dead so that's out as a distraction. I'm not one to watch anything unless it's sports, but I try. My dad is just as quiet as I am. I'm not really sure what to say to him in a time like this. We both just sit here, stunned.

You always fear that something of this caliber

will happen, but you never actually think it will. My insides are knotted up, my stomach roiling. Vomit burns in the back of my throat.

"Nate?" I hear my name called and look to see who it is. "What are you doing here?" Amanda asks, walking up to me on a pair of crutches with her ankle all wrapped up.

Seeing her lifts my fog and brings a small smile to my face. "My mom was just brought in."

"Why, what happened? It's not her MS is it?" she asks coming towards us. I stand and hug her, unable to answer her question. The truth is we don't know what it was yet. Tears burn my eyes, and when I pull away, I shake my head. "They are running tests now to try and figure out what happened."

"Oh my God, I'm so sorry," she says.

"Thanks. How's your ankle?" I ask her.

"I'll give you two a minute," my dad says. "Nate, I'm going to grab a coffee, do you want one?"

"Sure, thanks, Dad."

"Please don't leave because of me, Mr. Wilcox."

"That's nonsense, dear. I need some fresh air anyway," he says and waves as he walks away.

"So how's your ankle?" I ask her again.

"It's fine. It'll heal. How are you holding up?"

I shrug my shoulders and look her in the eyes. I'm not sure how to honestly answer that question. Right now, everything seems to be such a mess. Sitting next to me on the bench, Amanda wraps her arms around my waist and holds on to me. I hold her back, resting my chin atop her hair and try to calm my crazy thoughts.

"Do you want to talk about it?" she asks me. I shake my head, holding her a little tighter. With Amanda in my arms, everything feels better. She has a way of calming me. Maybe it's because she's become my best friend in recent months.

"Wilcox," a doctor calls from the other side of the waiting room. My head flies up and I catch sight of my dad making a U-turn to head towards the doctor who holds the answers to our fate. I look down at Amanda as she smiles at me. "Go," she says and I kiss her cheek.

"I'm Doctor Rosette. I assume you are Mrs. Wilcox's family?"

"We are. How is she?" my dad asks.

"She's resting. Her body has had a setback, if you may. There are many stages of Multiple

Sclerosis and a lot of patients regress and bounce back over and over. Right now, we are dealing with her first serious regression. It's going to take some time and some intense rehab to get her back to where she was. Her anemia is also really complicating the situation."

My dad and I look at each other, neither one of us knowing what to ask next. "I realize this is a lot to take in. She is very lucky that the medics got to her when they did," the doctor says.

"What does rehab mean?" I ask, wondering if there is anything that I can do to help with her rehabilitation. After all, I own a gym! And I can't just stand by helpless doing nothing.

"MS is a tricky disease which attacks the central nervous system. Considering your mom's fall and the current state of her reflexes, I think walking again is going to be quite the feat. But we have some great facilities that work with MS patients, and I'm hoping we can get her into one nearby."

"Would she have to live there?" my dad asks.

He nods his head and rests his hand on my dad's shoulder. Then his pager beeps and he looks down at it. "Here's my card, if either of you have any more questions, day or night. I'm sorry I have to run, but it's an emergency."

The doctor jogs off and I can't help but feel like my heart is being ripped from my chest. My mom is the rock our family. She means the world to me, and after losing Arion, I couldn't bear to lose her too. A nurse approaches us and asks, "Would you like me to take you to see her?"

"Please."

Both my dad and I follow the nurse through the maze of the hospital. Finally she stops and I take a moment to prepare myself. I can see her through the thin glass of the door, she is sleeping so peacefully. My dad clears his throat, obviously holding back the tears as the nurse opens the door for us. We head inside and the second that we enter, she turns her head, looking over at us with tired eyes, but still her same happy smile.

"How are my two guys?" she asks in a hoarse tone.

"We're fine. You have to stop worrying about us, Barb. Let us worry about you, honey," my dad says to her.

She nods her head, tears welling in her eyes. We both pull up chairs sitting on opposite sides of her. Seeing her upset absolutely kills me, and the helplessness I feel brings a surge of panic. To try to squash it, I search for the strength to speak some words of comfort, to stay focused on what *she* needs to hear, while all three of us are clearly shaken and silent. But I keep getting flashes of her on that goddamn bathroom floor. I shake my head to clear the shit out of it – I have to be strong for her.

"Ma, you know everything is going to be okay, don't you?"

She shakes her head and looks at me, then my dad. "You don't know that, dear. It might not be. I fell in the bathroom and knocked myself out, in pretty spectacular fashion too," she jokes trying to bring levity to the situation. "Judging from this knot on my head. So who knows what's going to happen next."

Pain resonates on my dad's face. He just wants to make everything better and since he can't...that's a struggle for him. And for me, too. "I could have slipped getting out of the shower and had the same thing happen," my dad says. "These things just happen. I know it's hard right now to be positive, but please try. For me, for us?" he pleads, looking at me too with grief-stricken worry on his face.

She nods her head and moves her arm to

wipe the tears away. Jesus, she is slow, so extremely slow. It worries me. I've never seen her like this. I grab a tissue and stand up, wiping the tears away for her. She smiles at me and says, "Thank you, baby."

"Do you want to rest?" I ask. "You look tired, Ma."

"No, I want to know what the doctor said."

I look at my dad and let him take the lead on this. I can't be the one to break the news to her.

"It might be better if he tells you," my dad offers.

She glares at him and shakes her head, "No, Jeff, I want *you* to tell me." She's clearly agitated, and scared. I wish I could make this all better. Just make it go away.

"Okay." He exhales and looks at me before speaking, giving her the doctor's assessment. He tenses up before he gets to the part about her having to move into a rehab facility, and as I look at my mom, tears gloss over her eyes.

I can see how hard this is for him, and I notice he purposefully left out the part about her possibly never walking again. She's so down and vulnerable, and I can only assume he just doesn't want to take her hope away. I know I couldn't tell her that right now.

She begins to cry and shakes her head, "No, I want to go home, Jeff," she demands.

It kills me to see my mom so upset. I watch my dad unravel, both of us feeling out of control in this situation. "And you will, but for now, this is what we have to do to get you back home."

She closes her eyes, crying. "And what if I never go home?"

"No!" he yells, "Please, honey, don't say things like that."

None of us say another word. The room is haunted by silence and the fear that this might be the end of the normalcy that we've always known. Watching my mom and dad cry, I feel overwhelmed. After all that they have been through, this is not the end they deserve. I wish there was something I could do to help. But there isn't. Fury brews inside of me and pushes me toward my breaking point. To at least spare them this, I do the only thing I can. I leave.

CHAPTER 3

Driving home, my insides are a twisted mess of worry and pain. My mom means so much to me, to see her so weak and suffering, it's…well, it is indescribable. My mind starts to swirl just like when I found her, and I do my best to stop the images. I can't go back to that place. The darkness starts to creep into my thoughts, and I just want to hold it off, but it's almost impossible. I focus on what my therapist has taught me. Coping with the aftermath of trauma is hard, especially learning to trust that I won't be totally overwhelmed by my feelings, that I can, in fact, handle it. I try to remind myself of this and take another deep breath.

Glancing down at my phone, it's still dead, so I plug it in to charge on my drive home. It's the first moment I've had away from my mom and it's hard to leave her. But I had to get out of there before I exploded.

My phone turns on and a text from Amanda comes in. *I hope your mom is okay. Call me.* Dammit, I feel terrible for not saying goodbye to her. I have to call her back; she'll be worried if I don't.

Watching the cars on the road veering around me, I realize how slow I'm going and how zoned out I am. My phone rings and I answer it without even looking at the screen.

"Please tell me you can come over," a familiar sultry voice says on the other end of the line. Pulling the phone away from my ear, I look at the screen, and sure enough, *Andrea.* Fuck. *Now* she calls. Why not last night when I was horny as fuck and only had my hand and some online porn to get me off? *Before* all this chaos.

Ever since I fucked her at Nash's birthday party last year, she's been riding my dick non-stop. She knows all I want is sex, so it's a perfect arrangement for me. I take a minute before responding to her, thinking if there is any way that I can make it work. But there isn't, and I know what my answer has to be.

"Nate, are you there?"

"Yeah, sorry. It's…I can't tonight."

Telling her no kills me since she never turns me down.

"Please don't say that, I am so fucking horny for you. Can I come to you or we can meet at the gym?"

"I can't, my mom's in the hospital."

"I'm so sorry. I'm such an ass."

"It's okay. You didn't know. Let me get through this and I'll be in touch."

We hang up and it pisses me off that I can't just go to her. She's become my own personal Arion in a fucked up way. She gives me a small dose of what I used to have with Arion and I fucking love it. Andrea looks so much like Arion and that's got me hooked. Watching her blonde head as she blows me or when I fuck her from behind puts me back in Arion's control for a few minutes at a time. So, sex with her I can't ever seem to get enough of. She's so sexy and a bit damaged like I am, which turns me on. Besides the obviously fucked up headspace of using her as my Arion replacement – I get it...it's twisted – there's the problem of her boyfriend. I don't love being the other guy, but it does help that he's a real douchebag, treating her shitty, talking down to her, and having his nose stuffed into fucking video games all the time. I don't get why she stays with him, but it works for me, since I'm not looking for anything serious. We just don't get time together whenever we want which sucks.

Putting my car in park, I head inside my parents'. Knowing what I have to do first, even though I don't want to…I have to. I grab a trash bag, paper towels, some cleaning shit and head upstairs, then I take an old towel out of the linen closet. Before walking into the bathroom, I take a deep breath, letting all the pent up air out of my lungs. I will my brain to take me anywhere else, to ignore the task at hand. My mind keeps playing tricks on me as it's pushing me back to that nasty room where I was held captive. I block it away, like I have so many times and just start to clean. But my mind gets the best of me and takes me back…

It's hot – fuck it's hot – and I can barely breathe. Looking around, the room is dusty. There is no light except the sallow sunlight that shines through the cracks of the door and a few open holes in the ceiling. My body hurts. My hands are tied behind my back to my legs. Dammit, I'm hog tied, like a fucking animal. Having my control taken away from me shoots panic through my heart. I thrash my body every which way, trying to break free and realize suddenly that I got one of my legs loose.

Before I can act on this revelation, I hear voices. It sounds like two men on the other side of the door. I quiet down and listen, but they aren't speaking English and my Farsi is not good at all. Ignoring them, I roll to my side to get a better look at how I am tied. If I got one leg free so easily, I can certainly do the rest. All my energy is focused on getting the hell out of here. Looking behind me in the dim light of the room, it's hard to make out what I'm seeing, or maybe it's that I don't want to see it. I move my leg to be sure that my eyes aren't tricking me and they aren't. My left foot and lower half of my left leg is gone. All that's left is a bloody stump, wrapped in God only knows what. The shock of realizing that a piece of my body is gone causes me to scream not only in anger, but in pain and confusion…

I pull myself out of that pain and find myself kneeling on the bathroom flooring, breathing rapidly, clutching a dirty, bloody rag. Startled, I look around and realize the bathroom floor is clean. Shaking my head, I walk the trash bag out to the cans on the side of the house. On the way back in, I happen to hear my phone ringing in my car. I grab it and see it's Amanda. "Hey, how are you feeling?" I ask, beginning to collect the things I need to take back to the hospital with me.

"I'm sore. But that's not what's important. How's your mom?"

"She's okay. The fucking prognosis sucks, but she's alive and that's what matters."

"What did they say?" she asks as I search for my mom's extra glasses in her nightstand.

I give her the lowdown, feeling another wrench in my gut as I do.

"Damn, Nate, I'm sorry."

"It's okay. I'm sorry I left you at the hospital, I should have said goodbye."

"Don't even sweat it. I needed to get home and elevate my foot anyways."

"You think you'll make it into work tomorrow?" I ask, finally finding the glasses. I grab her Kindle and a few more things on the list as Amanda talks.

"I don't know, maybe I'll swing by to grab my calendar. I'm going to have to cancel on some clients."

"No, don't do that. I'm sure Nash and I can figure it out."

"That's nice of you, but you don't do private sessions."

"I would for you."

"Knock it off. You'd probably push them so hard they'd fire me. I have a friend that can cover for me. If you don't mind I'm gonna call her and see if she can finish out my classes this week and I'll reschedule my individual clients."

"Whatever you say, you're the boss."

She laughs. "Technically you are, but whatever."

"Shhhh, don't tell my ego that. It'll go straight to my head."

"Oh yeah, I forgot about that ego of yours. It's the size of Jupiter and totally uncontrollable."

"You really do know me well. I'm gonna grab dinner for my parents. Do you want me to bring you anything?"

"Nah, honestly I just took a pain pill. I'm gonna crash, but I'll see you tomorrow."

"Sounds good. Lock your door."

"It's locked."

We hang up and I like that she's listening to me. She lives in a shitty part of town and for some reason thinks she's untouchable. Maybe the kickboxing classes she teaches have gone to *her* head.

Sleeping in a hospital chair might be the most uncomfortable thing I've done in a long time. Checking the time, it's 4:46am. I'm up before my alarm so I turn it off and watch my mom sleep peacefully. Her eyes are resting unworriedly, and I hope they stay that way. There isn't an ounce of pain inside of her at the moment. That's how it always should be. But when she wakes, that won't be the case. Thinking of what her body is going through starts the anxiety rolling through my body. My throat tightens and the nausea settles in the pit of my stomach. I so wish I could take some of it away.

Overtaken by worry and exhaustion, I fall asleep. Jolting back into consciousness, I check the time – I'm now running late. I hop up, not bothering to change for work, and kiss my mom's hand before bolting – I absolutely cannot be late opening the gym. Once on the road, I'm relieved traffic hasn't started yet and I make great time.

Parking, I fly up the stairs and get the morning started. Things get going and time flies. My mind is blissfully blank. Maybe it's because I'm busting my ass without Amanda here. Usually she handles everything on the floor. I'm more behind-the-scenes. But today it's all me, as Nash is booked with back to back training sessions.

I finally get a few minutes to breathe and reality sets back in. I step out and call my dad. He sounds exhausted. "How are things?" I ask him, leaning over the railing of the stairs that lead up to gym.

"The same. I'm actually going home to sleep for a while. Your mom is making me."

"Of course she is. Do you want me to go over there when I get off?"

"No, I won't be gone but a few hours. She was going to get more tests done when I left. You should rest."

"Are you sure?"

"Yeah."

"Okay. Any news on the rehab facility?" I ask him, noticing Amanda pulling into the parking lot.

"No, not yet, but I'll text you as soon as we hear."

We hang up and I head downstairs as Amanda's car door opens and her big black boot hits the pavement next to her sleek back Nike running shoe. I can't contain the laugh.

"I'm digging the boot, it looks good on you," I tell her.

"Don't be an ass, Nate."

"For real, I like how you've matched it with your black Nikes that you always complain hurt your feet."

She sticks her tongue out to me and I pull her into a big hug. She yelps in pain and I release my hold. "Be gentle with me, you fuck."

"Sorry."

"It's fine. How have things been here? Is Olivia doing okay?"

"Yeah, she's been great. Thanks for getting someone to cover."

"Of course."

We walk in and she heads to the studio to grab her calendar. On her way across the gym, I notice a few guys staring at her ass while she walks. If they only knew. "What's up, man?" Nash asks, out of breath as I glare at the assholes that are ogling Amanda.

"Nothing. Are you cool if I get going?"

"Of course, you've been here since the ass crack of dawn. Thanks for covering," he says.

"Any time." Just then Amanda emerges and he laughs out loud. "You could have told me that she stopped by."

"She just got here."

"And now you're leaving?" he teases me. Nash thinks that there's something going on with Amanda and I. "That's convenient."

"That's got nothing to do with me leaving. I've told you before that we're just friends."

"Whatever. Let me know how your mom's doing," he says and gets sidetracked by a client. He waves to Amanda as we leave, and I grab my car keys on the way out.

"So you really are leaving?" she asks, pulling her sunglasses down off the top of her head.

"Yeah, I'm starving. I was gonna grab a bite and shower before I go back to the hospital."

"I'll come with you; I'm hungry too," she says.

"Sure, where are you thinking?"

"Virgilios?" she offers and I agree that it's the perfect place to grab lunch.

"Sure, hop in. I'll drive."

"I can drive," she responds.

"Get your gimpy ass the fuck in the car, Amanda."

She rolls her eyes at me but listens.

As I back my car out of the parking spot, she doesn't wait two seconds before she turns in her seat and gives me a very serious look as she blurts out, "I saw Savannah last night."

"What?" I glance at her in surprise, before putting my eyes back on the road.

"I'm sorry, I know I told you I wouldn't but…I couldn't help it. She called and I was bored and all loopy from the pills and—"

"Do you hear yourself right now? Imagine if I went running after Arion every time I was bored. For fuck's sake, after all of the shit that she put you through, I can't believe you gave her the time of day."

"Come on, Nate, it's not any worse than you fucking that whore who reminds you of Arion."

I glare at her, I can't believe she even went there. "This isn't about me, Amanda."

"I know. I'm sorry, Nate, but I just can't say no to her."

"Why not?" I ask her point blank, so pissed that I'm about to pull my car over so we can get to the bottom of this.

"Because," she responds, aggravated.

"Because," I retort back, trying to get why

the hell she gave in to such a twat.

"I dated her for three and a half years. We have a past together."

It pisses me off to hear Amanda defending someone who betrayed her the way this chick did. Their entire relationship was a lie. The rage that so often seems to be just below the surface is suddenly stirred, and I can't bring myself to say anything else for fear of losing my temper. At this point, I'd almost rather take her back to her car.

"Don't be like that," she says.

"I can't help it."

"Then talk to me about it. I told you because I'm just as pissed at myself for giving in to her."

I take several deep calming breaths and try to keep myself in "sure-I-can-be-a-supportive-friend" mode, beating down "enraged-soldier-with-issues" mode with a fucking stick.

"Did you hook up with her?"

"God, NO! Give me a little credit, Nate."

"Okay, sorry." We pull up to Virgilios and I opt to valet because of Amanda's leg and because the kid probably makes just pennies per hour. If I can drop him a few bucks, then it's worth it. *See? Not a total asshole.*

We get seated right by the window and both of us take a moment to look over our menus. I look at Amanda – she deserves someone so much better than Savannah. I get that the breakup has been exceptionally hard on her, but every time she seems to be getting past it, she gets sucked in again. And I keep telling her if she'd just come out of the damn closet, then she'd have a hell of an easier time finding someone to be with and wouldn't feel that Savannah is her only option.

"Wanna split a pie?" she asks me.

"Sure."

"What do you want on it?"

"I don't give a fuck, you know that."

Amanda orders our lunch as I devise a plan to keep Savannah out of her life for good.

"Why are you looking at me like that?" she asks.

"I'm not looking at you like anything. But I do have a question – can you tell me what it was again that broke you two up?"

She's on to my game.

"Oh, that's right. She cheated on you, I totally forgot and with who?"

She shoots daggers at me before answering,

"My ex."

"Listen, I love you, Amanda. You're my best friend and I'll do anything for you. That's why it pisses me off to see you give in to this chick when she's a good-for-nothing whore."

"I know; that's why I told you I needed some perspective. I shouldn't have even thought about answering her call."

"Next time she pulls this shit, or tries to, just call me. I don't give a fuck if you tell her that we're dating. Whatever it takes. Don't waste your time again with her, okay?"

CHAPTER 4

"Are you gonna work out with me today, you pussy, or are you bailing?" I berate Nash, needing a good workout to relieve some of the pent up stress.

"Fuck you," he jibes back, punching me in the shoulder, making me laugh. "Don't forget who got you where you are today."

"Oh, I haven't. I owe everything to my mom." He shakes his head at me and we both chuckle, turning to Amanda as she approaches us with a smile on her face.

"I bet Amanda will work out with you. I told you, I got shit to do today."

"Nash, don't be an ass," Amanda chimes in. "Nate's going through a lot."

"Then work out with him."

"Sorry, I can't. I have a doctor's appointment today," she says, staring between the two of us. "Are you guys fighting again?"

"No," Nash blurts out as I simultaneously say, "Yes."

"What's the problem then?" she asks crossing her arms over her chest that is covered by a very tiny red sports bra. From there, I can't stop my eyes from trailing down her abs which are sculpted to perfection. She's really gonna make someone happy one day.

"Nash won't work out with me," I tell her, playing up the whiny bitch in my voice, but trying to be as serious as possible. We love fucking with her.

"Nate, for real," she says, trying to be helpful in her approach. "Look at all of the people in here, you don't see everyone working out with someone else, do you? You'll be okay, just go at it alone like you do at home."

I look around pretending to be very sad, 'cause if I look at Nash, I'll lose it. I can almost hear him laughing under his breath. Then I turn towards her with the saddest look on my face possible. She looks back at me and I can see that she feels terrible, but it lasts only about two seconds before I crack. Both Nash and I bust out laughing, pissing Amanda off immediately. She storms off and I yell, "Come on, Amanda, we were just joking."

"I actually felt bad for you, you asshole!" she shouts back, leaving out the front door.

Here at Mechanical Gym, we love to joke around, and for some reason, Amanda always seems to be the brunt of the jokes.

"That was fucking good, man," Nash says.

"Right? I love getting under her skin. She's so easy to piss off."

"For sure. Are you ready to lift some weights, you bitch? Your arms are looking a little scrawny," he glares down at my ripped biceps and I can't resist flexing them. To be in the kind of shape we're in, you take things to a whole other level. But regardless of whose arms are bigger, I do owe a lot to him. He's become a great friend and business partner and pulled me out of a depression that I was wallowing in. If it wasn't for him pushing me and giving me a purpose to focus on with this place, I don't know where I would be.

When I lost Arion, I thought I couldn't go on with my life. Everything halted when she chose Bain over me, but Nash forced me to move on. It's still a work in progress...sometimes a very fucked up work in progress…but hey, it's progress.

I grab my gallon of water that I've been slamming all day and follow Nash to the free weight area. "What do you want to start with first?" he asks me.

"Bench press?" I suggest.

"You sure? We did arms yesterday."

"Yeah, my leg is kinda sore…I'm not sure this new prosthetic is fitting the best."

"Have you called your doctor?"

"Yeah, I'm waiting to hear back," I tell him, grabbing a few plates and sliding them on one side of the bar while he does the other.

"How much do you want on here?"

"Two-sixty." We load the bar and I put my lifting gloves on and then lie under it.

"Ready?" he asks.

I nod my head and lift the weight straight up, then take in a deep breath as I lower it down to my chest. As I push the bar back up, I exhale, sweat beads on my forehead. I do this six more times before Nash helps me guide it back on the holder. *Damn, that was easy*, I think to myself as I lie there and rest before my next set.

"Did I tell you I found a ring?" he says out of nowhere.

"When are you gonna ask her?" This is huge for Nash – he's wanted to propose to his girlfriend Jess for a while now, but he's wanted to talk things over with her dad first and finally just got his blessing.

"I don't know, I was thinking on her birthday. She wants to go out of town, so she won't really be expecting it, but I hate to leave everything here on your shoulders, man. Especially with everything that you have going on."

"Dude, don't even worry about it. I need to keep busy. Spending so much time at the hospital is driving me a bit mental. I'm happy to pick up the extra slack if it means you going away and finally getting your ass engaged. Plus, I'll have Amanda back to keep my head on straight if anything hits the fan."

"Ohhhhhh, you and Amanda are so cute."

"Whatever, dude."

Holy shit, it feels so good to be home. Today's been one hell of a long ass day. I worked fourteen hours straight. My leg is so sore, and my body just needs to relax. Plus working out with Nash always exhausts me.

Sitting on the couch with a beer in one hand and a bottle of tequila in front of me, I flip on the TV, just as my phone beeps. I glance down at it, and it's Andrea...again.

She's been blowing me up tonight. Apparently the douchebag is at some sort of video game convention. Who even knew they still had shit like that? As much as I'd love to bang her, I'm fucking spent, besides being too drunk to drive. Plus, she already met me at the gym and blew me in my car today, so I can wait another day.

Opening the bottle of tequila, I knock back another shot, then text her back, ***Sorry, babe, I'm drunk off my ass. Raincheck?***

I'll come pick you up, she texts me right away.

Fuck! I lean my head back and flip on ESPN, looking for some good sports news that will take my mind off of her. Glancing down, my cock is hard. For real? A fucking text is going to get you going? The sports reporters are talking basketball, blah blah blah. Then a highlight from a game comes on and right away, I see Arion sitting courtside. Dammit. I go to change the TV, but I can't, I just keep watching as they show

Bain dunk the ball and her jumping up cheering him on. She's still pregnant and as gorgeous as ever. Then he winks at her, jogging down the court and I feel sick. Why can I never turn away?

Angrily, I click the TV off and snatch my phone, texting my address to Andrea. I take another swig of tequila to numb the pain.

Want me to pick you up? she texts me back.

I snap a picture of my dick and send it to her.

No, I'm alone. I'll fuck you here.

It's not but ten minutes 'til there is a knock on my door. I take another shot and walk over ushering her in. I look outside to make sure no one saw. With her crazy ass boyfriend, who knows what he's really doing? The street is quiet, and there are no unfamiliar cars.

"Hi, gorgeous," I tell her, closing the door. My head is spinning, but I know what I want. She walks away from me to set her purse down and I see Arion, like always. I wait for her to come back to me. Closing my eyes the second our bodies touch, my mind is consumed with Arion.

"Jesus, I missed you," she says crashing her lips against mine. I growl in response slamming her body against the wall. Her fingers find my pants before I can do anything else, and just like that, she has me in her hands stroking my shaft with the same eagerness Arion used to. I keep my eyes closed, imagining I am with Arion again.

The biggest resemblance between these two might just be the way they suck a dick, and boy, does Andrea love to suck me off. She drops to her knees pulling my pants down. As she kneels, I brush the hair gently out of her face. Her lips mold around the head of my cock and I thrust myself into her, making everything I was thinking about wash away. Yeah, I might not be with her for the right reasons, but she is using me just as much as I am using her.

My earlier exhaustion is now replaced with an eagerness for her, to please her and in return find the same pleasure myself. But before any of that can happen, I stay in this moment, where I am right now. My body feels heady, my need to come so strong that I want to give in, wanting to show her how good of a girl she is and to also relish in one of the world's greatest gifts.

Since returning home and losing Arion, I've moved on the best that I can – if it can even be called that – and in doing so, I've become obsessed with sex and everything it entails.

Maybe it's because I went so long without it, maybe it's because I'm older now and am no longer ashamed to give into what my body desires, or maybe it's my way of avoiding the risk of real emotions, not wanting to get hurt again the way Arion crushed me. But whatever it is, if given the opportunity to come all day, I would.

Fuck, she's good. All of a sudden, my body quavers as I brace my weight against the wall, tilting my head back. She stops sucking for a second and jerks my cock vigorously. "Come for me, Nate. Give it to me," she orders, and right away, I let go. She places her lips around my head and sucks up every last drop of what I give her. I can't control my noises – never can. But, it's one of the things that gets her wet. Andrea is very vocal herself, and it's such a turn on. I also love that she tells me what she wants.

Looking down at her, I get a flashback of Arion. This happens so often when I'm with Andrea, and I have to admit it's what keeps me coming back. I still need those glimpses into the life I had with her. As much as I miss the times we had together. She's moved on and I need to as well, beyond just looking for the Arion experience with other girls. The problem is…I

can't. This is all that I can handle right now –
sex. And…Andrea gives me that. I'm not looking
for the strings of a relationship, not with my past
or my problems.

She pulls away and I help her stand, then
draw my pants up. "Do you want a beer?" I ask
her.

"Sure," she says, following me into the kitch-
en.

"Here you go, babe," I say as I hand her the
beer, standing square in front of her.

"Why do you call me 'babe' and 'gorgeous'?"
she asks.

I run my thumb over her bottom lip before
answering and watch her melt looking up at me.
"'Cause that's what you are?"

"Jesus. I really wish we could make us work,"
she says.

"I know you do, but anything more than
what we have will change everything. I'm not
boyfriend material."

She shakes her head and I can see it hurts her
when I tell her no, but I'm not letting my guns
down on this. So I distract her how I know to do
so well. Taking my hand, I run it across the small
of her back and around her side. Her breathing

quickens as I trail my fingers up her stomach to her breasts, where I go in, grabbing a handful of her plump tit. She moans, resting against the counter, and I lift her shirt, kissing her nipple before I take it in between my teeth.

She almost falls back, catching herself at the last second, then slowly, she lowers herself. I smirk at her as she lies back so beautifully against the cold counter. Taking my hands, I lift her up and trail kisses all over her body. Her arms are splayed so beautifully above her head, showing every contour of her body. She reaches down and unbuttons her jeans. I know what she wants, after all, it's why she's here.

Taking my hands, I slide them under her waistband and she lifts her ass so I can get them off. Her pussy is glistening for me, so wet and beautiful. Looking at the counter she is lying on, this is perfect. I can fuck her here and not have to worry about my leg one bit. Pulling my pants down, I grab a condom out of the pocket. She leans up, watching me roll it down my length, and the second I'm done I ask her, "How do you want it?"

"Hard. Fuck me as hard as you can," she says with the most serious expression on her face.

Looking down, I line up my cock with her opening before slamming into her. She screams out in ecstasy arching off of the counter and I pull her thighs down, getting her right where I want her. Everything inside of her is tight, I'm so fucking horny it's hard to even describe. She wiggles a little above me and it spurs me to begin moving, deep, long, hard strokes, hitting her in just the right spot.

"Take your shirt off," I pant, needing to see her tits bounce while I fuck her.

She listens like a good girl, even removing her bra. So finally, I give her what she asks for – a good hard fucking. It rubs my cock off just right and I can sense that I can come again. Andrea is lying there bracing her weight, holding on to anything she can as I fuck her intensely. Her noises are so loud, matched with my grunts, so I know it won't be long 'til we relish in a release.

Looking down, I love how my cock looks, how sexy it is to watch myself penetrate her body. Focusing on her sex wrapped so tightly around me, I lose it. With my hands fiercely gripping her hips, I revel in yet another orgasm and am rewarded with hers as well. Her entire body shakes, she has one hand clamped around her tit while the other is on my side, willing me to keep going.

Looking down at Andrea, I see Arion. I close my eyes, tilt my head back, and let my fucked up mind drift me to the past so I can keep the illusion of still being with Arion alive.

CHAPTER 5

"I really wish you'd stop worrying about me," my mom says, doing her best to stay strong.

I can see she's worried herself; it's written all over her face. She keeps picking at the skin on her arm and that's how I know. She keeps leading on that everything is okay, but I can tell she's only telling me what I want to hear, to make me feel better. My dad is still talking to the doctor outside the room and I can't bear to leave my mom right now.

"I'm not worried," I lie, hoping it will calm her a bit.

"Nate, you have the same look on your face as you did when you broke the Neilson's window when you were seven, or when the cops came to the house for the party that you weren't throwing while your dad and I were out of town, or—"

I cut her off, "All right, I get it. I'm worried, Ma." Images of her in a nursing home as her health declines race through my mind. "I mean, how the hell am I not supposed to be, Ma, when you're the most important person in my life?"

"You have to trust in the doctors and have faith that they are sending me to the best possible place there is."

"I'm trying, I really am. But you're going to be almost an hour from the house, we can't stay the night with you, it's…it's just a lot to process."

"I know. It'll all work out, baby, you'll see."

I let go of her hands, placing my face in mine, exhaling deeply, while I do my best to listen to her words and really believe in them.

My dad walks in with the same expression on his face that he's had for a week now and it's clear the news today crushed him. "Dr. Harrington believes this place you're going is the best in the state."

"See, Nate? I told you they are sending me to the best place there is."

"Will you stop saying they're sending you away? It's like you're getting shipped off and we're never going to see you again." I feel bad for snapping at my mom, but my tolerance for all this worry is wearing thin. Besides, I'm protective of her, especially since losing Arion.

"You know what I mean." She reaches for my hand and my dad's too. All three of us sit in silence, not saying a word. There is a sense of fear amongst us for what the future holds.

"How long do you have to be there for?" I ask.

She looks at my dad with tears in her eyes. I already know what the answer is. *They haven't given her a timeline.* It all depends on whether or not she can regain her strength and walk again. My mind starts to spiral…what if she never walks again? Immediately, I fear the worst and have to excuse myself from the room. I take a breath on my way out, to keep myself in the moment and in control. Emerging into the hallway, the doctor is still out there talking to one of the nurses. When I'd talked to him earlier, I'd felt the information he was giving us was really vague. He looks right at me and asks me, "How are you doing?"

I shake my head, "I don't know."

"Can I help?"

"I'm not sure how to say this, but what if my mom's MS gets worse, or if she can't bounce back from this?"

He takes his glasses off and rests a hand on my shoulder. "The course of the disease is different for everyone. Right now, it's too difficult to predict what will happen, so my advice is to be positive for your mom. It'll make a difference in her recovery, enjoy every single second that you have with her, and don't let your mind drift down a negative road."

I nod my head, understanding how he handles things, but I on the other hand am a realist. Don't get me wrong, I'm trying to be positive for her…but there is still that constant fear inside of me that she's never going to come home.

"I'm trying, I really am," I tell him genuinely. "But aren't there any other facilities closer to here that she could get into?"

"For your mom, it came down to treatment options. In just the past week, I've seen a decline in her health. This place handles MS patients vigorously, and they have the best of the best rehabilitation specialists. I promise you all are going to love it. The drive not so much, but her treatment is worth it."

"Okay," I agree.

He shakes my hand and says, "Remember, call me any time if you need anything at all."

He walks off and I look around, feeling everyone staring at me. Rage courses through me suddenly, and I want to blow my hand straight through the fucking wall. Instead, I take a deep breath, knowing I need to get out of here and have a drink…or five.

Walking back in, my mom is asleep…well, at least her eyes are closed. I gesture my dad towards me and he listens. As we step out into the hallway, I give him a hug. "I'm so sorry, Dad."

He just nods his head holding on to me; my dad is so broken. Pain burns in my chest because I've never seen him this upset. *Goddamn the situation we are in.* "She's gonna be all right, dad." I try and comfort him, but right now my attitude sucks, being here isn't going to help anyone or anything.

"Nash called, he needs me to stop by the gym, if you're cool with that?" I lie, looking for my escape.

"It's getting late, son, please go."

"Thanks," I tell him and glance in at my mom once more; she is still sleeping just like an angel.

I call Nash as soon as the cool air hits my face.

"What up, sexy?" he answers being a smart

ass, but it brings a smile to my face and convinces me that getting his perspective on things will help.

"Just leaving the hospital. Wanna meet for a drink?"

"Sure, where are you thinking?"

"The Tavern?"

"Sounds great, I'll see you there in about fifteen."

I hop in my car, my mind racing with a million different things swirling through it. I'm really not sure how my dad and I are going to handle being so far away from my mom, or how she is going to cope with being off somewhere on her own, without us. In a time like this, she's going to need us more than ever.

While I drive, I can't think of anything to make things work. All I keep picturing is her on the bathroom floor and I sure as hell don't want that to happen again.

Pulling up to the bar, it's busy. There are tons of people crammed inside, so I decide to head in and grab a spot at the bar while I wait for Nash. Luckily there are two spots right at the end of the counter, which I swoop and then try to decide what to order.

Since I need to be able to drive home to-night, I decide to stick with beers, but my nerves make me want a shot. I can always call Amanda to pick me up…she doesn't drink…so when the bartender comes over, I order two beers and three shots. As she sets everything in front of me, I hand her my credit card to open a tab and knock back a shot. The cool burn of the alcohol and the warmth in my stomach is my favorite.

"What up, brother?" Nash asks, sitting next to me grabbing one of the beers. "Is this for me?"

"Sure is," I tell him, grabbing mine.

We clink bottles and he asks, "How are things?"

"Not good."

"Didn't get the news you were hoping for?"

Shaking my head I take a swig of my beer. "No, maybe even worse."

"What? Why?"

"The hospital is moving her to a facility an hour from our house and the doctor won't even be frank with me about the prognosis."

"Can you get a second opinion?"

"We did. The other doctor agreed that rehab is the best thing for her."

"Damn, man, I'm sorry," he says.

"Me too," I tell him and knock back another shot, he does the same, and fortified, I admit my fear, "I don't know what to do, man."

"Is there anywhere else that she can go?"

I shake my head as the bartender approaches. "We'll take another round," I tell her.

"Why don't you move closer to the place she's going? I'm assuming that it's going to be long term?"

"Yeah, I'm pretty sure it is."

"You've been wanting to get your own place for a while now, this will just help you make it happen. I bet Amesha could find you something sick and pretty quick."

"That's not a bad idea. You got her number?"

"Hell yeah, I do." He pulls his ginormous phone out of his pocket and scrolls through his contacts. "I'll text it to you."

"Thanks."

"I'm glad you asked me to meet. I wanted to talk to you about the whole..." he looks around the bar to make sure no one we know is there. "The engagement."

"You still thinking her birthday?"

"I am, but with everything that's happened with your mom, I completely understand if you want me to stay in town for a while."

"Absolutely not. Book your trip, and ask her. Amanda will be back at work soon and I need to keep busy."

"You sure?"

I grab a shot and slide one to him. As much as I'm hurting inside for my mom, she's going to be okay. I have to believe that. Right now he needs me to step up, and he's helped me so much. It's the least I can do. "To the future," I toast. We raise our shots to each other and leave it at that.

CHAPTER 6

"How's the ankle feeling?" I ask Amanda.

"It's good. I'm ready to start teaching classes again, that's for sure."

"When are you thinking?"

"I was gonna try next week, but with no weights or anything."

"Make sure you tell Candace and just take it easy, okay?"

She glares at me, she's tired of me babying her.

"Hi, Nate," an unfamiliar voice says from behind me. I look over my shoulder to see a cute brunette standing with her hands on her hips.

"Hey," I respond and look at Amanda. She has a smile on her face and I know exactly what she's thinking. I'm hesitant to turn around. Most of the women that come up to me here are after one thing…my money. But I will myself to turn anyways. Being the owner, I don't want to be an asshole, in case this chick really does have a legitimate question. She continues to stare at me with her brown hair and big eyes. I can see right through her contacts that they aren't really blue.

"Did you have a question?" I ask her.

"Oh, yeah…sorry. I was…I was wondering if I could book some private lessons with you?"

Immediately I shake my head. "No can do, I don't give lessons. But Amanda does." I turn to see her still watching us. "Isn't that right, Amanda?"

"Sure. Wanna take a look at my calendar?"

Then the chick completely catches me off guard stepping to me, touching our bodies together and wrapping her hand around one of my biceps. "Please," she whispers, looking up at me with the most pitiful eyes.

Before I can react, Amanda jumps in, saving the day. She separates us and wraps her arm around my waist. "The only one he gives lessons to is me. Got it?"

As I hold Amanda back, I chuckle, especially watching the way this chick changes. "I'm sorry, I had no idea you two were dating."

"Well, now you know," Amanda retorts.

She turns and walks away, clearly embarrassed. I turn to Amanda with a huge grin on my face. "Thank you," I say and give her a hug.

"I'd do anything for you. You know that."

"Thank you, I just never thought pretending to be my girlfriend would be one of them."

"Dude, I saw the way your body tensed when she came at you like that. I read you well."

My phone rings interrupting us and I glance at the screen to see an unfamiliar number on it. "I'm gonna grab this." I step away from the counter for a little privacy since it could be related to my mom.

"Hello?" I answer as I head outside.

"Is Nate available?"

"Yeah, this is him."

"Hi, Nate, this is Elania, Amesha asked me to give you a call about your interest in buying a new home?"

"Oh great. Thanks for calling me so quickly."

"Did you have time now to tell me a little bit about what kind of house you're interested in?"

"Sure, I've never done this, so…I don't really know."

She laughs a little and says, "Don't worry, I'll show you the ropes." We chat about some basic specs, then I give her my email address and we hang up. For the first time in a while, I'm excited. Having a place of my own would be unreal. I've never had that, and as hard as it is to imagine doing it without Arion, I have to. She is not my future anymore.

I'm doing this for my mom and for myself. It will be nice to have my own home. My phone rings again and I glance to see my dad's name on the screen.

"Hey, Dad?"

"Hey, how are you?"

"Good, just working. How's Ma?"

"She's good. The staff at this place is great; she was wondering if you were still coming for dinner?"

"Of course. Will you be there tonight?"

"Should be."

"Great, well, text me and let me know if either of you need me to grab anything on my way over."

I hang up with my dad and head upstairs. If buying a home is coming sooner rather than later, I guess I need to educate myself on what I really want. Amanda is talking to someone and Nash is giving a lesson. I'm not really in the mood for making rounds, so I head into the office and get online searching for homes in the Scotch Plains area.

One townhome looks really nice. I click on it and right away, my attention is diverted to the listing agent's picture. Damn, she's fucking hot.

Dark hair and intense eyes paired with those soft lips and huge tits popping into the picture. Man, I wish she were my realtor. I'd fuck her in a heartbeat, based solely on this picture, and that's not like me, I like my Arion-blondes.

Then I read her name: Elania Harmon. Holy fuck, she *is* my realtor. I can't get involved with someone right now. However, my questioning is all washed away as I get lost staring into her eyes again. What's wrong with me? I can't remember the last time a non-blonde was able to get me going.

But those eyes. And lips. And tits.

"Whatcha looking at?" Amanda barges in and asks me.

"Fuck, you scared me."

"Why? You watching porn?"

"Fuck no."

"I'm just messing with you." She leans on the desk and looks down at me. "For real, what are you doing?"

"I was just looking at houses."

"Yeah? Did that realtor call?"

"Yeah, she did."

"Have you found anything good yet?"

I decide I might as well show Amanda what this chick looks like. I have a feeling I'm going to be needing her advice having to work with her through this process. "Just this," I tell her, turning the screen and pointing to Elania's picture.

"Who the fuck's that?" she asks, basically drooling.

"The goddamn realtor."

"Damn, Nate, she's hot."

"Tell me about it."

"Is this what has you all hot and bothered in here?" she asks me, crossing her arms over her chest.

"No," I lie. "But it does have me excited to look at houses, that's for damn sure."

"Can I come too?" she asks jokingly.

"Why? So you can hook up with her? What kind of friend are you?"

"I'm just playing with you."

"Riiiiight."

Having told my parents about my plans to move and have them both excited for me is such a relief. Dinner with them was great. My mom seems to be doing really well. Even though she's only been at the new facility a short period of time, it's great. All of the staff really seem to care about her.

Leaving them, I have one stop on the way and I can't wait. Andrea texted me—the douchebag is out for the night and I really need to fuck her. Just thinking about her naked body waiting for me turns me on like nothing else. My cock throbs as I make the trip across town.

Finally, I pull up to her place and will my cock to stay down, just long enough for me to walk in. My phone chimes with a text. It's from Amanda, *I checked your realtor friend out and guess what?*

Dammit, I hate it when she does this shit, just tell me. ***What?*** I text her back.

She's single, doesn't appear to have any kids, and loves to work out.

How the hell did you find this shit out?

Facebook.

You're a piece of work, you know that, right?

I did it for you. Well, really for me…I was mayyyyybe hoping she was gay.

I don't text her back. Would she really steal a girl that I was into? She's my best friend and friends don't do that shit. I shake away the thoughts and get out of my car, looking around to make sure no one sees me before I slink my way inside.

The door is open like she told me it would be. She's naked and in the kitchen making us drinks. Locking the front door like it's Fort Knox, I walk towards her, taking the drink out of her hand. This chick knows how to make me happy – her naked ass and a stiff drink.

"Hi," she says, looking at me through heavy lids.

"Hey," I respond taking a drink and running my free hand through her hair and then down her body.

She shivers from my touch. I love how eager she is. I pull her body tightly against mine, holding her to me with force.

"Did you miss me?" I ask. She nods her

head. "Why don't you show me?" I push my erection against her and she drops to her knees, fumbling with the button and zipper of my jeans. Once my cock is free, she licks her lips holding my shaft in one hand. I nudge myself towards her, urging her to suck me. She doesn't waste a second. Her warm mouth engulfs the head of my cock. Just like Arion did. Yeah, once again I think it's wrong to use Andrea this way...but I can't help it. Slowly she moves up and down, her soft warmness making me so hot, just the way Arion used too. *Dammit, I can barely stand it.*

As she picks up speed, her hair falls into her face and I move it out of the way. Holding it back so I can watch the way her mouth stretches around me, I know she won't stop 'til I come. Don't get me wrong, I want to, but her pussy sounds so much better. Pulling back, I will her to stop. She fights me by clamping her lips tighter. I keep pulling and when we disconnect her lips pop.

She smiles up at me and I help her stand. Leaning down 'til we are eye level, I glide my fingers over her hot cunt. Her body shudders when I begin to rub back and forth.

"Where do you want me to fuck you?" I ask.

She doesn't answer me, instead she stares at the muscles of my chest, clearly fixated on my body. I sink a finger inside of her and she looks at me, dazed and horny.

"Anywhere," she murmurs and I grab her ass cheek, squeezing it hard between my fingers. She giggles, twisting out of my grasp and runs into the extra bedroom. I follow and lock the door behind us, watching her get situated on the bed. She has her ass up and face down. I can't stop myself from stroking my dick as I observe her. She's so hot. Ivory skin, like Arion. Blonde hair, like Arion. Light eyes and the best tits in the entire world, just like Arion.

"How long do we have?" I ask, taking my pants off and rolling a condom on.

"A few hours." Typically I cut the time given down in half. As much as I think her boyfriend is a good for nothing asshole who I'd love nothing more than to beat the fuck out of, I don't want Andrea to reap the repercussions of him finding out. He's been physical with her in the past and I'm sure will do it again.

I step to her. She is playing with herself, but I nudge myself against her pussy. She's so wet and ready. The instant we touch, she drops her hand

and backs into me. I fill her sweet pussy, going all the way in, she's so wet. She moans out, throwing her head back and resting up on her hands.

I start to move, pulling and pushing myself into her. I love the way her body accepts mine, meeting me thrust for thrust. My insides are on fire. Closing my eyes, I tilt my head back and smack one of her ass cheeks. Doing my best to not leave a mark.

"Yessss!" she cries out in ecstasy.

My balls tighten from her words. The sensation of my cock is so much to handle. Everything inside of me pulsates with every movement as our bodies crash, together bringing us so close to climax. Shuddering from head to toe, our worlds collide. She screams into the pillow and lets go as I follow suit, almost screaming out Arion's name while I get lost in the moment and the daydream of fucking her yet again.

Fuck, something's wrong with me. I recover quickly and lean down, leaving a few kisses on her back before pulling out. Then I head into the bathroom to flush the condom. It's the best way to get rid of the evidence and ensure that the douchebag never finds it.

Walking back into the bedroom, Andrea is

still lying on the bed. I put my pants back on and lie next to her. She scoots over and puts her head on my chest. I don't want to be a dick, but this is where things get weird for me. I know she wants more, she's told me – she's asked me. I'm not ignorant; it's the reason that she keeps sleeping with me. She hopes that things will pro-gress…but with Andrea, they can't.

I'm using her just as much as she is using me. To me, she is a dose of Arion. She gives me a little bit of what I lost, and I'd know if I *was* ready – which I'm not – I wouldn't move on with her. I couldn't start a relationship out on the circumstances that we have. I would always look at her like she is Arion and that's not fair to either one of us. Sick as it might be though, there's a part of me that just wants to take whatever I can get to relive the best days of my life.

I pretend my phone vibrates and sit up to check it, then I turn to her. "I gotta run, I'm sorry, babe."

She kneels behind me wrapping her arms around my neck. "It's okay, thank you for coming. I'll miss you."

I kiss her cheek and get up. On my way out, I wish to God that she really was Arion.

CHAPTER 7

"Have you started looking at houses?" my mom asks me.

"Not in person, but I'm actually going today."

"That's great, dear, I'm so happy for you."

"Thanks," I tell her, noticing how good she is looking. "I heard you took a few steps in physical therapy the other day."

Her face beams from my words. "I did! I couldn't believe I was able to, considering how I've been stuck in this wheelchair, but I put my mind to it."

"You can do anything you put your mind to, Ma."

"I'm not giving up. So tell me what kind of house you want?"

"I'm not picky, you know that. Anything that is close to here will do."

She laughs, only the way my mom can, and

looks at me with that look. "You better think about it, Nate. Buying a home is a huge purchase and I don't want you to do it for me. I won't always be in here"

I love her optimism. It reminds me to stay positive. "I agree, and I know you won't. Nash and I are looking to open a second gym and we've talked about this side of town, so this is where I wanna live, and for now…I'll be closer to you."

There is a knock on the door and a nurse pops her head inside. "I'm sorry to interrupt you two, but it's time for your physical therapy, Mrs. Wilcox."

"That's okay. Mandy, come in. Have you met my son yet?"

The young girl shakes her head at me and I can see where this is going. My mom is trying to introduce us for reasons of her own. "Nate, this is Mandy, she's one of the nurses here."

"Nice to meet you," I say and stand to briefly shake her hand.

Instantly she becomes shy, turning to the side and pushing her hair behind her ear. As much as I love my mom, I don't want to get caught up in her shenanigans, or make poor Mandy feel any more awkward than she already does, so I kiss my mom on the cheek and bail.

Plus, I have to meet Elania at her office to go look at houses. Since seeing her hot ass picture I can't stop thinking about how she's going to be in person. She gave me clear directions to her office, and was precise in saying not to be late. I guess we have a schedule to follow. I don't really care about all of the details, as long as we find me a place that's close to my mom.

Plus, my dad's job typically has him travelling to meet with clients. Lately he has been postponing that, but that can't go on forever. Checking the directions in my phone again, I make the last few turns before pulling into the parking lot of her office. Checking the clock, I am early, but decide to head in, considering how strict she was with giving me orders to not be late. It's hot as a bitch outside, and I, of course, decided to wear jeans. It's not that I'm embarrassed of my leg, I just don't want to explain it to her the first day I meet her.

"Hi, welcome to New Age Real Estate, who are you meeting today?" the perky receptionist asks me.

"Elania Harmon," I respond looking around

the contemporary office.

She glances down at something on her desk then asks me, "Are you Nate?"

"I am."

"Have a seat, I'll let her know that you are here."

I give her a slight nod and turn to see four white leather chairs. I take a seat on one of them and suddenly feel nervous. I'm not sure why, so I pull my phone out and aimlessly keep busy with that. Then I catch sight of a blonde walking by, but it's not her. My eyes keep wandering, so curious to see Elania. Then I see a pair of shiny black heels talking to the receptionist. My eyes scan her body, long legs, tight ass, and quite a substantial rack.

Her hair is straight and just completes the entire package. Too bad she's not Elania…I can tell 'cause her hair is different. Fuck, she's smoking. I'd love to fuck her. As I watch her, I imagine peeling that dress off of her tight skin. I would move my hands over every inch of her.

Then she turns around and with those light eyes, I realize right away it *is* Elania. My heart pounds against my chest, and I will my cock to stay calm as she struts towards me. She has such a confidence about her that I…I'm speechless. Each step that she takes, so strong, that I feel it through the floor.

"Hi, Nate, I'm Elania, it's nice to meet you."

I stand and shake her hand. "It's nice to meet you, too," I respond. I have a hard time keeping eye contact with her, as her body distracts me.

"If you're ready, let's get going," she says.

I nod my head and look at my dick…for Christ's sake. I do my best to think of anything else as we walk out. "It's hot today," she mentions and walks up to a red Cadillac Escalade. I'm impressed that this is what she drives, it's such a big car to handle.

"It is," I reply before we get inside.

"So you still like the list I sent you?"

I nod my head, not understanding why she has this effect over me. "You don't talk much, do you?"

"I'm sorry, I just have a lot on my mind."

"No need to apologize. I'm a talker, so if I bug you, please let me know."

Pull your shit together, Nate. "You're not bugging me. I'm sorry. Maybe I need to eat lunch or something."

She looks over at me as we wait to turn out

of the parking lot. "We can."

"I don't want to inconvenience you."

"It's not an inconvenience at all." She glances at me out of the corner of her eye. "I didn't eat much myself. Plus, I found a few other places I'd like you to look at that we could possibly bump up to today?"

"Then we should eat," I tell her.

She looks at me for a second before asking, "So tell me, where should we eat?"

"What about the Gem?"

"I love that place," she responds.

"Good." My phone rings and it's Amanda. I knew she would pull some shit like this, especially since I was nervous to meet Elania. I'm sure she just wants to know how things are going...but now is not really the time to start discussing that.

"You can get that if you need to," Elania says.

"Nah, it's just work. It can wait."

"What do you do?"

"I own a gym upstate with a friend."

"Really? What's it called?"

"Mechanical Gym."

"No way. I've heard of it. I actually looked

into becoming a memb—"

I cut her off. "Why the hell haven't you?"

"The location." She smiles answering me. "It's pretty far from where I live," she says stopping at a light. She glances in the rearview mirror and I can't stop myself from completely staring at her. Her legs are something else. So long and smooth, paired against the stripes of her dress make me want to touch her.

"We've talked about a second location. Just tell me where you want it and I'll make it happen."

She laughs and glances at me. "Really, just like that? I tell you where I want it and you'll build me a gym?"

Watching her repeat those words out of her sexy mouth makes my cock grow. I will eventually have my way with her...I can guarantee you that.

She speaks again, pulling me out of my lust-hazed reverie. "I live in Scotch Plains, where you are looking to buy, so considering we might be neighbors, anywhere by your new place would work."

I think about living close to her and it does something inside of me. Maybe it's because all I want right now is to be close to her. To touch her, to feel her, to taste her, and to please her.

"Here we are," she says interrupting my daydream again.

The valet opens her door and I stall for half a second watching her get out. *Christ, I'm such a fucking creep.*

"Do you come here often?" she asks me, as we head in. I hold open the door for her.

"Only once, just for drinks."

"They have the best food, so you'll love it, I'm sure of it."

"I'm sure I will," I respond dryly, suddenly feeling nervous again.

She talks to the hostess then asks me, "Are you okay sitting in the bar?"

I nod my head. Honestly, that's my preference, seeing as I need a drink or two, just to take the edge off.

The hostess takes us to a high-top table in the middle of the bar, and being a gentlemen, I pull Elania's chair out for her. I don't dare try to push it in though, considering how high the table is. She'd looked like a little kid being sat by her parent.

Glancing over the menu, the food does look

really good. I decide on a burger and my favorite, a beer. Elania pulls a folder out of her purse and sets it in front of me. "This is what we have scheduled today, but these two listings just popped up on the market, I think we should see them too," she explains, pointing at the listings as she talks.

I glance over the two new listings then look up at her. "We can see whatever you want...you're the boss."

"Nate, this is up to you. *You're* the boss."

Hearing her say those words turns me on. I readjust myself and take a drink of my beer as the waitress sets it down in front of me.

"Can I ask you something?"

I nod my head, watching her delicate hand hold on to her glass of red wine.

"Why are you buying a house? When you don't seem to care much about the details."

I exhale and lean back, wondering if I should tell her about my mom. I barely know her, but figure I'd rather be up front now. "I'd like to be close to my mom. She's having some health issues and needs me right now."

"Nate, that is very sweet of you."

"Thanks," I say, wondering how to change

the conversation.

"Have you been in real estate long?" I ask.

"Not too long. But it's always been my passion, so I'm happy to finally be doing it full-time. What about the gym? Is that what you've always wanted to do?"

I smirk at her and love how easy the conversation has been between the two of us so far. I swear she almost melts when I look at her like this. "Nah, not really. I kinda stumbled into it. My buddy needed some financial help, so I agreed to partner with him."

She smiles again, processing what I'm saying, and I realize how apropos it was to say I stumbled into the gym. Hell, when I agreed to help Nash, I had one leg and was a wreck. Thinking about it, "stumbled" might actually be the perfect way to describe it.

The waitress sets our food down, and I realize then that we both ordered the same thing. "There is no way you are going to eat all of that," I tease her.

"The hell I won't," she says far too loudly.

"Wanna bet?" I ask.

I can see the seriousness in her eyes; she is absolutely going to eat every last bit of it. I shake my head and dunk a few fries in some ketchup, getting ready to sit back and watch the show that Elania is about to put on for me.

CHAPTER 8

Oh fuck. Fuck. Fuck. Her lips are so good. I can't stop my hips from moving as I knot my fingers tightly into her hair, basking in pleasure. I get lost in her movements and her noises. My hand finds her dress and I clench her cunt, before rubbing vigorously back and forth on her sweet spot. She's not wearing any panties, and quite frankly, that doesn't surprise me.

She pulls away and looks up at me. "Can I fuck you?" she asks.

I nod my head and watch her open the center console, pulling out a condom. *Such a good girl.* Looking around, the parking garage is empty, and thanks to her tinted windows, no one could see in if they wanted to.

She tears the package open with her teeth and I roll the condom on. Then she straddles my lap. Her hot pussy hovers above me as she looks intently into my eyes with need…a need I can fulfill. Waiting for her to move is excruciating.

"Kiss me," I order, knowing that this will get her body to go. The second our mouths connect, she whimpers, giving in. My cock slides effortlessly inside of her. Taking my hands, I brace her hips. But I don't move her. I sit back and let her work.

My body is full of so many emotions. From spending the day with Elania and my perpetual half hard dick, to stressing about my mom, to craving only Arion to make it all better...my mind is simply fucked up. Which is how I found myself calling Andrea, which I never do, but I got desperate. I needed her to clear my mind, and now here we are in the parking garage of her work, my Arion fix bouncing on my dick while I'm still replaying things over and over in my head.

Checking the clock, we don't have long. Closing my eyes, I imagine Arion on top of me and let her move. Her pussy, so warm, and she faintly sounds the way Arion did. Reaching my hand under her dress, I find her tits and squeeze hard, then move to her nipple. She moans in liking. "Yes, Nate, touch me."

Watching what my cock does to her as she

works me by herself moves my body to the edge. Then it hits me, and I let go, bucking my hips under her. The instant I grunt out in pleasure, Andrea screams herself, coming along with me.

Finally I open my eyes to see she is smiling at me, so sexy with her messy hair from my hands playing with it. I laugh a little when I try to tame it. She leans into my touch and says, "Leave it, that way I'll remember this moment when I look in the mirror."

Alarm bells go off yet again at her words. Lately she has been getting clingy, saying little things like that, insinuating that we should be together. Don't get me wrong, she's amazing and all…but beyond the Arion look-alike bit, she's just not someone that I am looking to move on with. Hell, I don't think there is anyone that I want to move on with.

"You gotta get back to work," I tell her. Typically I call her "babe." It's just a habit…I guess…or the more fucked up truth, if I'm gonna be honest with myself, is that it lets me disconnect from her enough to keep her in Arion mode. Jesus, I am such a mess. But now I wonder if it's led her to think I want more. I wonder about a lot of things, worrying about more things than I should, and sometimes I drive myself crazy with the constant mindfuck and the what-if's.

As Andrea readjusts herself, I remove the condom and drop it outside of the door. "I liked you calling me," she says. Another sign this was a mistake.

"I know. But I won't make a habit of it; I don't want you getting caught. There's a reason you haven't left…"

I trail off because I don't remember the douchebag's name.

"Ronnie."

"Yeah, 'cause you haven't left him."

"I would if—"

I cut her off. She knows better than to start with this and if she wants to continue what we have then she needs to stop with all of this talk about us getting together. "Andrea, you know I'm not looking for a relationship right now. I have too much baggage and some really deep shit to handle. So please stop with the insinuations about us, okay?"

She nods her head and there is a little look of crazy written all over her face.

"Take a few days and make sure you can

keep your emotions out of it and if so…call me. If not, thank you for everything. You are truly an amazing girl."

Tears gloss over her eyes and it's definitely time to leave. Leaning over, I kiss her on the cheek and get out of her car, walking the few steps it takes to reach mine. I get in without looking back and drive off. I don't want to seem heartless, but I can't give Andrea what she needs, and if I was with her, it would only be to fill the void in my heart that Arion left.

My phone rings, and it's Amanda…again. I answer through the hands-free headset. "What's up?"

"Nathaniel Jeffrey Wilcox, you better have a damn good excuse for not calling me back today."

I chuckle at her attempt to sound mad. "You want the truth, or should I bullshit you?"

"What the fuck do you think?"

"Calm down, you know that fake ass mean doesn't work with me."

"It's not fake; I'm pissed."

"Come on, I was just going to call you. I got busy with…well, I got busy—"

She cuts me off, "You were with that skank

again, weren't you?"

"She's not a skank. What's your problem with her anyways?"

"I don't have a problem with her, it's just…I don't like cheaters after what I went through with Savannah."

"I hear ya. Speaking of which, have you heard from her?" I ask getting on the freeway.

"Yeah, she's been up my ass."

"Have you seen her?" I ask with irritation laced in my tone.

"Hell no, but she wants to."

"I'm sure she does. Don't let her guilt you at all."

"I won't. I promise. So how was the realtor?"

I exhale thinking how to handle answering the question.

"Nate, are you there?"

"Yeah, sorry. She was good."

"Hah," she laughs. "That's it? She was 'good'?"

I think about it again. Amanda is my best friend, she's one of the only people in this world that I trust. If I'm going to tell anyone about today, it's her. *How can I say this without sounding like a creep?*

"Just tell me already."

"Okay. Being around Elania had my dick at half-mast all day, and the thoughts that crossed my mind as we looked at houses were not...gentlemanly."

"Meaning?"

"I wanted to fuck her every which way, in every single room of every house that we saw. She's un-fucking-believable."

She chokes on something and begins to cough. "I'm sorry," she says through a strangled gasp. "Give me a minute."

"Please don't say something smart," I warn her.

"I won't. I'm just processing this and wondering why you didn't just fuck her and instead fucked that skank."

"I don't know. Elania's not that kind of girl. She deserves more, and quite frankly, if I get to fuck her, I want it to be more than once."

"Whoa...more than once? Shit's serious. Sounds like you're getting over Arion, maybe?"

"I don't know about that...but I'm excited to look at houses again tomorrow."

"Why tomorrow? You looked today. You got it that bad?"

"Uhhh, we ran out of time. We had lunch and planned to look at a few new ones that just came on the market. But we didn't get to them, so we're going tomorrow."

"Lunch? You just met her."

"And I was starving."

"You're always starving. It sounds like you went on like three dates with her already today. Shit's getting super serious!"

"Why are you being such a brat?" I ask.

"I'm not, I'm sorry, it's just Savannah has me stressed and I'm—"

"Taking your anger out on others?"

"Haha, I'm sorry. But it really is a big deal that you're even hesitating from having a quickie with this chick…it's progress, Nate. I just want you to be happy."

"Enough with the sappy shit! Now, do you want me to pick you up and we can go hit the punching bags at the gym?" I ask her.

"You can pick me up, but what if we go out and have a few drinks instead?"

"I can do that, too."

One word Amanda said rings in my mind, "progress"…am I making progress in getting over Arion? Maybe.

CHAPTER 9

Fucking Amanda. I'm blaming her for this. My head is throbbing and I don't want to move. My phone beeps and I check the time. I have to get up. I don't want to…but I have to. It beeps again and I check Amanda's messages. It's a picture of me getting a lap dance from some chick at the strip club last night with a *Thanks for last night* text.

I can't believe I let her talk me into drinking so much, although we did have a blast. It got me out of my own damn head and it took her mind off of Savannah too, which is all I wanted. Yeah, I feel shitty today, but oh well. It was worth it. Plus there's nothing I can do about it now.

The shower calls me to wash away the scent of cheap perfume and alcohol. A combination that neither my therapist Roger nor Elania would appreciate. I'm not really feeling like talking to Roger today, but if I cancel, he'll call, and I'd rather just get it over with now. Before I get in the shower, I check my email, wondering if Elania sent any new listings.

Sure enough, there are two.

To: Nate Wilcox
From: Elania Harmon
May 14, 2015 5:53am

Hey Nate,

I've scheduled the two listings we missed yesterday for today. Also, here are a few more new ones that I thought you might be interested in. Let me know if any of these look good and I'll add them to today. Should we grab lunch afterwards this time, so we make all of our showings? :)

Elania

Before looking at the attachments, I go right into her next email.

To: Nate Wilcox
From: Elania Harmon
May 14, 2015 6:37am

Here are a few more. :)

I'm not really sure what to say. I don't want to sound like I am completely desperate for her. I decide to call her office, this way I can hear her voice. And I'll get a feel for the day.

"May I speak to Elania Harmon, please? It's Nate Wilcox." I ask the receptionist.

"Please hold," she says.

Glancing at the clock, I'm cutting my time short, but this is worth it. While I'm on hold, I put my prosthetic on and then head into the kitchen to grab a power bar and a glass of OJ.

"Hey, Nate," she answers in her usual chipper tone.

"Good morning, I hope you don't mind me calling."

She laughs a little, "Not at all."

"What's so funny?" I question her, wondering what I said that made her laugh.

"It's far from morning, Nate, that's all."

"Maybe for you, getting up at five a.m. and shit. I had a late night."

"Well, we all don't work at a gym. I've got to get up early to get my run in."

I love that she takes care of herself. It's so sexy.

"Then I'll let it slide."

"Thanks, did you have a chance to look at my emails?"

"Absolutely," I lie to her. I never opened the attachments. "That's why I'm calling, I…I loved them all, but I'm not sure if we'll have time today to see every one of them."

"That's great. I'll schedule what I can for us today, then we can go again tomorrow, if you want?"

I agree, knowing it's going to be tough to make a decision on buying a place, for the simple fact that all of this will end. I hear her reception-ist in the background, "Elania, I've got Rachel on line three."

"I gotta run, Nate, but I'll see you here in a few hours." We hang up and I head into the bathroom. Fuck, I don't want to shower, I'm so sluggish. I turn the shower on and wait while the water heats up, almost falling asleep it takes so long.

After I am cleaned and dressed, I take a few Tylenol and Ibuprofen. I'm tempted to take a shot as well, but Roger will sniff it right out of me. On the drive, I call my mom to check in with her. Everything seems to be going well. I told her I'd stop by tonight and I could tell it made her day.

Now sitting in the waiting room of Roger's office, I look at all of the books that line the walls, and wonder why all of these are out here in reception. Then again, what's it matter to me? Tilting my head back, I close my eyes, exhaling deeply. I wonder what he'll ask me today, or what he'll want to talk about. I guess I should bring up what happened with my mom. He needs to know and can help me deal with all the shit that's come flooding back to me.

I've tried to take this seriously, but things have become so mundane that when he asks me the same questions repeatedly, I lie. I'd stop if I could, but the military still has a hold on me, at least for a little while longer. The clock on the wall ticks, second by second, so slowly, and I know as soon as it strikes noon, he'll open the door. I wonder what he'd do if I went in there early? I wonder how he lives his life so OCD and controlling that the clock directs him the way that it does.

"Nathaniel," he welcomes me in right on time and I just smirk at him, shaking his hand as I enter. "How are you?" he asks me.

"Good." I've learned not to ask him how he

is; he's made it clear that this time is for me. We both sit, him on his boxy square armchair and me lying back on the lounger.

"So…have you done everything I asked?" he questions me.

"Of course."

"You haven't been drinking?"

"Not one bit," I blatantly lie.

"And you haven't been looking up Arion and Bain online?"

I shake my head, embarrassed that at one point I did become a bit obsessed, but at least this answer is honest. And that *is* progress.

"So what's new then? It sounds like things are going really well."

"Well, not really. My mom's health isn't doing so well," and I explain what we've been going through with that. He looks genuinely sympathetic, and I do appreciate that about ol' Roger.

"I'm sorry to hear that. How does that make you feel?"

"Helpless. Like I just can't do shit for her when she needs me most. It's fucking awful."

"What else?"

"Angry. I found her when she'd collapsed and it was really hard to see her that way."

"Did it trigger any flashbacks from Afghanistan? Or otherwise?"

"It was a combination of everything: Arion, the war, and then really morbid thoughts of my mom."

"I see," he says to himself, taking methodical notes while we talk. "Have you been practicing your breathing exercises?"

"Yeah."

"Good. Why do you think you hold on to that moment with Arion so much?"

"I don't know, probably because I feel responsible. It's the same with my mom. Since I've been working so much, I wasn't home to take care of her. Maybe, if I was there all day, I could have noticed the signs of her body declining."

"You need to know that what happened with your mom is not your fault. You don't have a crystal ball. You make the best decisions you can in each moment with the information you have right then, and you can't be angry with your past self for not knowing what the future would hold."

I adjust myself in my seat and nod my head, doing my best to process his words.

"Nathaniel, you're a fixer. You take on everyone else's problems to try and make them better. It helps you give the illusion of control and makes you feel safer, but it's not really control. While in the process, you're only neglecting yourself and what makes you happy."

"It's how I've always been, I put others first…plain and simple."

"Have you noticed whether you're more that way since coming home?"

"Maybe. Probably," I admit.

"Then what about you?"

"I'm fine."

"Until you're not, then what?" I shrug my shoulders. "You've had to work really hard to get past the aftermath of what happened to you. I'd hate for you to have a setback because you're too busy worrying about others, opening yourself up for your symptoms to come roaring back."

"I won't." I snap. "I don't want to relive being treated like an animal, beaten, starved, and tortured, all right? I think I'm doing fine on my own."

"Nathaniel, please trust me on this."

"I'm sorry, Roger, I can't."

He nods his head and drops the subject – for now – but given a little more time he'll bring it up again. How is putting others first a fucking crime?

"How's your sleep been?"

"Good," I lie. Knowing it's only from the liquor, and if I'm not drunk, I don't sleep for shit.

"Are you taking the Ambien Dr. Remington prescribed you?"

"Nah, I haven't had too for a while now."

He stops writing and looks at me. Like he's reading into what I am saying.

"Are you still seeing Andrea?"

"I am."

"Is she still with her boyfriend?"

I nod my head. Roger doesn't agree with my decision to be with her, and is the one that called me on my bullshit in the first place, seeing how I was using her. Quite frankly, sometimes I don't agree with it either. But my dick wants what it wants and I'll tell you my hand is not enough to satisfy it. Plus, her boyfriend is a goddamn loser. At least this is the shit I tell myself.

"Nathaniel, may I be blunt?"

"By all means," I egg him on.

"What is the point of your life?"

I stare at him shocked. The old bastard has

some fucking nerve.

"That's what I want you to think about until our next visit. What is Nathaniel Wilcox's purpose in life?"

CHAPTER 10

That man has some motherfucking balls. Driving to Elania's office, I'm agitated and could use a drink. His off-the-wall statement just keeps ringing in my head. *What is the point of my life?* Fuck, if I only knew, I sure as hell wouldn't be seeing him. Why do I need to tell him anyways? My purpose is my business. I do my best to let it go, but still in the back of my mind, it nags me.

Pulling up to Elania's office, she is standing outside and looks pissed.

"You're late," she barks at me.

"I'm sorry, I had an appointment on the other side of town and I didn't take traffic into account. I should have called you."

"Yes, you should have."

There is a flame in her eye and I like it. "It won't happen again."

"Good, you can drive today," she says walking to the passenger side of my car. She's in another one of those damn dresses and I'm not sure if I can handle the skin of her legs rubbing all over the leather of my seats. But I can tell she's not joking, so I unlock the doors and let her in.

"Where to first?" I ask starting the car and looking over at her.

She's squinting looking through a file of papers on her lap. "I've got the whole route plugged into the GPS of my phone. It'll tell you where to go." She clicks start and the GPS begins to direct me.

"So this first place is one of the new listings from yesterday. The other one got a contract, so I pulled it from ours today."

I keep listening to the GPS and her, doing my best to stay focused. My cock is starting to throw me off, but I fight it away.

"I told you, you're the boss. I'm just along for the ride."

She smiles and says, "This one is a townhome, three bedrooms, two and a half baths. It's right by a new shopping development, so the area has some great growth potential."

"Does it have a garage?"

"Of course."

She seems to have calmed down and I feel the need to apologize. Clearly I pissed her off, though I didn't mean to. I don't want her to think that I'm not taking this seriously, or I don't value her time, because I do.

"I'm sorry about earlier, it won't happen again."

"It's all right. I'm sorry if I came across wrong. I've just had a stressful day."

"It happens. Wanna talk about it?"

She shakes her head and I can tell that she's just like me. I've been talking for months and months and it hasn't completely healed me. Instead it's left me more stumped if anything. Now, I have my psychologist questioning the reason for my existence, or "purpose" as he likes to call it.

"Here we are," she says as the GPS stops. The area is nice, and the home is definitely newer. We get out of the car and I look up at the beige colored home. I could definitely see myself living here.

"I know what you are thinking – the garage is attached around back."

"I wasn't thinking that," I respond as I follow her up the front steps. *I was thinking that I'd like to fuck you.* But, that's normal lately.

I love looking at houses with Elania. The passion that she shows for her clients is something else, clearly this is what she was born to do. And it's obvious how smart she is, how driven, how much of a perfectionist, and it's all sexy as hell.

"There's no maintenance here, everything is taken care of for you by the homeowner's association," she says unlocking the front door.

We head inside and I'm a bit taken aback. This place is way over the top, new wood floors, granite countertops, dark cabinets, and the entire floor plan is open. It's just...perfect. The attention to detail in the craftsmanship is off the charts. Elania shows me everything, somehow already knowing all of the features of the house. I can tell that this is one of the reasons why she's so good at her job. I really try to listen, but then she begins to walk upstairs and following behind her is just about my undoing.

I almost act without thinking, I just want to touch her. My hands yearn for her body. But somehow...I stop myself knowing that I can't. It would not only make me look like an absolute creep, but it would definitely freak her out.

But if I could, I mean, if she wanted me, which she very well may…well, there's a countertop staring right at us, the right height for me to lift her up on. I'd slide her dress up and fuck her 'til she came on my cock.

"Did you hear me?" she asks looking at me as we stand at the top of the stairs.

"Of course I did," again I lie.

"Good, I'm glad you like it. I knew you would. The other two bedrooms are over here and there's two full baths."

We meander through the top level before making our way down to the garage. I really don't see anything wrong with this place. And it's only five minutes from my mom. The problem: buying something ends all of this with Elania. It's crazy to think that way, but it's the truth.

As we stand outside and take one last look, I try to think with my head and not my dick. "Wanna put an offer on it?" she asks.

"It is pretty damn perfect."

"It is, but we can look at a few more before deciding."

We spend the rest of the day following the map she had planned. House after house after house, and to be honest none of them compare to the first one. So I pretty much have no choice but to put an offer on it. I can't see a way to stretch the house hunting out, since the decision is so fucking obvious. Elania said the sellers have twenty-four hours to respond to my contract, which at least means I have a reason to look forward to tomorrow, knowing I'll be hearing from her. As I watch her walk back into her office building, it hurts. In such a short period of time, I've grown to like her. Maybe it's just my dick doing the thinking for me, but it feels like so much more than that. Something stopped me, something made me not make a move when I was around her. God knows I wanted to…but I didn't. And when I'm around her, Arion is the furthest thing from my mind. Which I cannot even believe. Zero comparisons. It's just all about Elania. Fuck.

"I put an offer on a place," I tell my mom as we sit and enjoy the pizza I brought for her.

"Oh, honey, that's great and really fast."

"I know, and it's really nice."

"Where is it?"

"Probably five minutes from here. I actually drove by you twice today while I was out looking."

She stops eating and looks up at me, "And why didn't you stop in?"

"Well, I was with my realtor. I didn't want to barge in here with someone that you didn't know."

"Thank you for considering that, but any time you are near, please stop by. I don't care who you're with."

"But—"

She cuts me off. "No, Nate, don't argue with me. This may be how I am for a while. I want to see you as often as I can, and I love your friends. So if they come, then that's a bonus too. Speaking of, how's that cute girl Amanda doing? Are you two still just friends?"

Hah, my silly mom. Does she really think I'd bring my realtor in here? A friend, yeah, but not someone I'm doing business with. "Yes, Ma, just friends."

She reaches for her water and is a little shaky. I hand it to her and worry that things aren't getting any better for her here. With all of the physical therapy, I would think that she would be improving faster. Her mood is good, at least, she's in great spirits every time I see her, but there's only so long that she can keep up with it if her body doesn't get any better. The usual panic starts to rise, but I push it down. She just has to get better. She has to.

CHAPTER 11

-Elania-

"Please tell me that you aren't working late…again."

I glance at the doorway of my office and roll my eyes at Jacquelle. *Like she cares.* She's one of the other realtors in my office, and a totally conniving bitch. "I'm waiting to hear back on an offer for a client."

"You know you can do that from home?"

"Jacquelle, I have shit to do. I'm up to my knees with work. So unless you have something of importance, please spare me."

She glares at me, a sliver of the setting sun rolls through my office window, catching her fake gold necklace. I don't know why she even bothers coming in here. I hate her and she knows exactly why. It's not rocket science. "Excuse me for trying to be nice," she says.

"I doubt that's what you were doing." She turns on a heel and leaves. I wish her goddamn heel would snap as she stomps down the hallway. I enjoy the image of her flying forward, face-planting, breaking her nose, and covering her face in gnarly rug burn. It's soothing, really. *Christ, I'm messed up.*

Since her mom owns the agency, she thinks she has some weight to throw around here, but I couldn't give two shits because she hit the top of my shit list the day she went after my man. The thieving bitch that she is had been eye fucking him for months. Not that he's innocent in it all, but now my hate is never gonna change.

As I run comps on a customer's new listing, my phone rings.

"This is Elania," I answer.

"Hey, Elania, it's Dan, I saw you put in an offer on the Highland property. But I wanted to let you know that they received another offer for ten thousand over the asking price. Do you think your client would come up? We need to know within the next ten minutes."

"Thanks for telling me, Dan. I'm not sure. Let me get a hold of him and I'll be in touch."

We hang up and I dial Nate, but he doesn't

answer. Checking the clock I know I have to get ahold of him now. I dial him again, but get voicemail.

I shoot him a text, hoping that I'll get a response.

Impatiently, I sit and wait. Running a search on new listings wondering if anything comparable pops up. I realize Nate loves this place and it was so close to his mom, so that'd be great. It's also right down the street from my house. I almost gasp out loud from the thought alone. *What is wrong with me?*

I stare at the screen, wanting him to text me back, but also not wanting to be overanxious. I can be like that. I decide to keep doing what I was in order to pass the time. Before long, my phone rings again. It's Dan. Shit. I let it go to voicemail. As I wrap up that last of what I have to do, Nate still hasn't called me. I decide to pack up and just as I'm leaving, he calls me. I answer it right away, excited to see his number on my phone. "It's about time."

"Sorry, I was having dinner with my mom."

"It's all right, I'm just giving you a hard time. Did you get my text?"

"I did."

"What do you think?" I ask him.

He exhales then speaks in his silky smooth tone, almost making me melt from it alone, saying, "You're the boss, you tell me."

"I think it comes down to how much you really want this place. I told the other realtor I'd give him an answer in ten minutes, so I'm not sure if we'll get it at this point.

"I love the place, I really do, El." He stops and corrects himself. "Sorry, I meant Elania."

"It's okay," I tell him. A delicious shiver had run up my neck when he called me "El."

"Do whatever you can. I'll pay the extra ten grand and then some."

"Ok, I'll put in a verbal offer for the new amount. If I need you to sign an amendment to the contract I'll be in touch. Keep your phone on this time, though."

We hang up and I dial Dan back. This part of the job is always so stressful, but I thrive on it. As soon as he answers, I explain what Nate is willing to give, hoping we made it, adrenaline buzzing.

"Didn't you get my message, Elania?"

"No."

"They accepted the other offer, I'm sorry."

Instantly, I feel deflated.

"Jesus, Dan, you couldn't have given me a little more time?"

"I told you ten minutes. The sellers were literally boarding a plane."

I get off the phone with him, finding it hard to believe that this deal fell through when it was all so right for Nate. My stomach is queasy. I've lost all my motivation tonight. I just need to get in a hot bath with a glass of wine and it's sure to calm me down. It's nights like this when I wish I had someone to go home to. It makes me miss Alex more than I realize. Maybe calling Nate, even though I have bad news to give him, will cheer me up. I do love his silky smooth tone.

Walking out, I'm the last one to leave. I flip off all the lights and exit through the back door. Getting in my car, I call Nate through my car's Bluetooth. This time he answers on the second ring. "Give me two seconds, El."

"Okay," I respond, and my ears perk right up. I can clearly hear grunting and am just a little shocked, wondering if he's actually having sex. That's both wrong…and a little hot? I'm tempted to hang up, but then I hear a guy counting. "Two more man, push it."

He's at the gym. But I'm picturing him naked. Shit.

"Eleven. Twelve." Then the clank of metal clear as day and I know I was right.

"Give me five," he says to whomever he is with. Then he's back on with me. "Sorry about that, I had to finish that last set and you told me to keep my phone on, so I answered."

"It's okay, not a big deal. You can call me back."

"No way, what's up?"

"Uhhh, not much." I stall not wanting to give him the news on the house. "Do you work out every day?" I ask him, picturing how well his shirts have fit him every time I've seen him.

"Yeah, try to. You really should come by sometime."

"I wish I had the time to. I'm actually just leaving work."

"See? And I'm just getting started so if I waited for you, we could work out together." *Is he flirting with me?*

"Are you offering me private lessons?" I imagine Nate standing behind me as I work out with him. *Jesus, he's hot.* I suppress those thoughts; I can't go there with him, or anyone. Not after what Alex did to me.

He laughs at my comment. "No, not lessons. But we could do some workout sessions together."

"Do you do personal training?"

"I don't."

"But for me you would."

"Dammit, El, why are you digging? Do you want to work out with me or not?"

"I do."

"Then let's make it happen." My heart thuds against the walls of my chest.

I'm a bit taken aback by his statement. I didn't expect for him to put me in my place. People don't usually do that. His tone is strong. Maybe he's not flirting, and he genuinely just wants to work out. Suddenly, I second guess everything.

"Okay, now, did I get my house?"

I can barely choke out the words, my mind is spinning from this man, but I have to. "No, we were too late."

"Damn, okay. When do you wanna look again?"

Someone bounces back quickly, I'm pleasantly surprised. "I'm driving home now, let me look at my calendar and I'll text you." He sounds genuinely excited to see me again, even if it's to look at houses; maybe he is into me. Not that it matters, I'm not ready to move on with anyone.

CHAPTER 12

-Nate-

As I deal with Andrea texting me again, I can't control my mind as it drifts elsewhere. Normally, I love an impromptu message from her about hooking up. But for some reason, tonight, I'm just not feeling it.

Maybe it's because I'm contemplating texting Elania back. She was supposed to let me know when we could go look at houses again and that was over three and a half hours ago. Something has definitely gotten into me if I'm watching the clock this way like a moony teenager and can't get my dick enthusiastic about a free fuck elsewhere. I'm sure she's busy anyways. As I knock back another beer, I watch Nash and Jess on the dance floor. He is so much bigger than her; they are such an odd couple. But the way she looks smiling up at him is priceless. I had that once. A pang hits me deep in my chest, and I shake my head to clear the thoughts. Not tonight, I'm not going there. I'm happy for my friend, and even though my fucked up brain always has me comparing myself to someone else, it's not fair to put Nash and Jess in the picture.

"What'd I miss?" Amanda asks me, coming back from the bathroom and throwing an arm over my shoulder.

"Nothing," I respond, shaking my head.

"When's he asking her?" she asks me.

"On their vacation, next week."

"She's gonna be so surprised. Did you give him any pointers?"

"Fuck no, I did that shit so long ago and you see how well it turned out. I'm the last person who should be giving him that type of advice."

The bartender comes over and I order another beer for me and a seltzer water for Amanda. She's not much of a drinker, which is fine by me, 'cause I always got a sober driver. As I turn to her, she has my phone in her hand and I lean over to see what she's doing. "When did this start?" she asks.

I snatch it away to see that Elania texted me. *Hey Nate, how about this weekend?*

I glance at Amanda who has that look on her face. The one that says *Why the fuck didn't you tell me, dickweed?* "Yesterday." She rolls her eyes at me, like I've been keeping it from her for a year. "I promise. I didn't even have her cell number 'til then."

"And?"

"And what?" I laugh at her. It's like I'm cheating on her or something with Elania.

"What's your plan?" she asks turning in her seat.

I shrug my shoulders. She knows damn well I don't ever have a plan. "The contract on the house I wanted fell through, so we have to go look again."

"And?"

"Why the fuck do you keep asking me that? And. And. And."

She punches me in the shoulder. "'Cause, I wanna know what's going through that head of yours."

"Oh, trust me, you most definitely don't wanna know."

"Try me."

"She's hot and I'd love nothing more to fuck her. But she probably has a boyfriend at home, or doesn't see me like that."

"And what if she doesn't? And does?"

"I don't know. She evokes things inside of me I'm not sure I want to let out. Plus, I got other shit to focus on, like my mom and—"

She cuts me off. "Nate, if she's making you actually *feel* something, then don't push that away."

The bartender sets another shot and beer in front of me. I guess I slammed that last one without even knowing it. As I turn the shot around and around in my fingers, one word Amanda said rings loud and clear, *feel*. Does Elania make me *feel?* There's something there and it's more than just lust. Since my mind has been drifting towards her, remembering our interactions, I've actually been blowing Andrea off. That's not like me, considering we've fucked for the better part of a year.

"I don't know what she's doing to me. I really don't."

"Well, text her back. I'm going to dance."

I nod my head. She knows I'm not a fan of being on the dance floor, aside from being a one-legged, gimpy ass freak-show.

Looking down at my phone, I re-read her

text.

I really don't want to wait 'til this weekend to see her. With alcohol coursing through my veins, I just start typing. **Got anything sooner?**

I do, but I want to see what new listings pop up on Friday. That's usually when new homes come on the market.

Okay, that works. In the meantime, you should come work out with me.

I pray she doesn't turn me down. I really don't want to sound desperate, 'cause I'm not, but something inside of me really wants to see her. Despite the panic that tends to start buzzing every time I think of letting her see even the smallest hint of interest, I need to see her. There's something so intriguing about her and for once not just my body wants her. But there's a mental connection – we click. And by whatever crazy miracle, it seems worth the risk of putting myself out there again. I think.

I wait to hear back from her as Amanda, Nash, and Jess leave the dance floor.

"Did you figure shit out with the realtor?" Amanda asks through heavy breaths.

Both Nash and Jess are drunk and making out next to me. "Her name's Elania…and not really."

"I know that, asshole, you know what I mean."

I roll my eyes at her, taking another swig of my beer. I'm ready to go home. I'm not about to have a heart to heart in the middle of a crowd. And I doubt I could handle that right this second anyway. It's enough for me to even let the thoughts shoot across my brain for a split second. Any more and I'd probably end up hyperventilating like a little bitch.

She looks at Nash and Jess, who are about to cross the line in public and says, "Let's go, I gotta get these two home."

We all load up and I don't say much to Amanda. I hate it when she acts this way, all controlling. That's *my* gig. After we drop off Nash and Jess, Amanda smiles at me, and I can see that she feels bad.

"Come on, Nate, I'm dying over here. I have to know what you've been texting."

"Not much really. We've just been talking back and forth." I'm hesitant to admit that I could really be moving forward in fear that it will jinx things.

"About?"

"I don't know, mainly house stuff and a little about ourselves."

"Does she know…" she trails off.

"About?"

She looks down at my pants and I can tell she means my leg.

"No, and it's honestly been the last thing on my mind."

"I've told you a million times a good girl won't care."

"I agree, no one looks at me any differently when they see my prosthetic, it's more of a quirk inside of me." Honestly, it's not my leg that really freaks me out. It's general rejection, my leg is just a good cover. Something that I can blame things on and hide behind.

"I get that, Nate, I really do. It's like me being gay – if I told the world, ninety-five percent of people wouldn't care, but I'm just scared."

"I know you are, but you shouldn't be. One day you'll tell the world," I tell her and lean over kissing her on the cheek. Knowing I need to listen to my own words just as much. "Thanks for the ride, babe."

"Any time."

As I head inside, I check my phone. There

are two text messages from Elania. *You never told me what working out together entails?*

Guess, I'll pass.

Damn, girl, I'm sorry, I was driving home and lost track of time. Working out will entail whatever you want.

I'm not really sure what we should do, since all I really do is jog. I guess you'll have to show me the ropes.

We could climb ropes, I tease her.

I'm not sure my arms could handle it.

I'll help you.

I wait for her to text back as I crack another beer, but…she doesn't. I wonder what she's thinking. Did I say something wrong? I'm sure I didn't. Checking the time, it is after midnight. Damn, now I feel really bad. She's an early riser and here I am bothering her.

I tilt my head back, letting the alcohol take me where it may. And for the first time in I don't know how long, it's not to Arion. All I see is Elania, dark hair, exceptional body, that laugh, and those eyes. If only I could know what's behind them. I sense that she's been hurt, hurt just like I have.

CHAPTER 13

-Elania-

"So are we still on for tonight?" my cousin, Mads, asks me as I poke my fork around my salad.

"Actually…I have to cancel."

"Elania," she scolds. "You promised me that we'd do this together."

"I know I did and I'm sorry, but something came up with a client. Plus, you know softball isn't my thing."

"So you're cancelling for the entire season?"

I nod my head wary of looking her in the eyes. She's getting married soon and really wants everyone in the wedding party to join this league. "Well…yeah," I finally admit.

"No, hell no, this was supposed to be for fun."

"And it still will be for you and Josh. Plus

you'll have everyone else in the wedding party there."

"I'm not doing it without you. Besides, what could be so bad about drinking and playing something for fun?"

"Oh my God, you're killing me."

"Pleeeeease," she says in such a wheedling tone.

"Uhh, fine, Mads, I'll do it, but not tonight."

"Deal. So what came up tonight anyways? What client?"

"Nothing unusual, just a meeting." Heat radiates to my cheeks as I sit here lying to her.

She scrunches her eyebrows at me and says, "Anyone who starts a sentence with 'Nothing unusual' is definitely lying. So spill it."

"I'm working out at the gym of one of my clients."

She almost spits her water out. "You're what?"

"You heard me." I glance around the restaurant sure that everyone is staring at us because of her outburst, but no one is.

"I'm sorry, but you can go work out with a client, have fun with a client, breach a professional line with a client...but you can't play softball?"

"This deal is really important to me."

"More than disappointing your cousin?"

I shake my head.

"Then bring your client to play. Obviously they are athletic."

"Come on, Mads."

"What?"

"Nothing. I'll ask him."

"It's a guy?"

"Yeah."

"Why did I not know this?"

"Uhhh, I didn't think it was important."

"Well, it is! Out of nowhere you're blowing me off for a *guy*. Client or whatever you say, but since that crap Alex and Jaquelle pulled on you, you've been a hermit."

"Can we please *not* go there right now?" Bringing up my past does nothing but hurt. Plus, working out with Nate is really for professional reasons anyways...or that's what I keep telling myself.

"Of course." She checks her watch. "I'm sorry, I didn't mean to bring that up."

"It's okay, it's the truth."

"After what you went through, I would do

the same thing. That's why it means so much to me that you join softball. You need to start getting back into social world."

"I appreciate the support, Mads, I really do."

"I'm always here for you, dear."

"Me too."

"Good, now I hate to say, but I gotta run to an appointment before softball."

She gets up from her chair and throws down a twenty-dollar bill. I give her a hug before watching her walk off. Mads really is one of the sweetest people in the world. She's just watching out for me and I appreciate that…I'm just all twisted up inside with this Nate situation and trying to figure out which end is up with him. As I dig into my wallet for the other half of the lunch bill, I think about asking Nate to softball.

Would it be weird? I wonder how he'd feel. I'm hesitant and second guess it. Letting my nerves get the best of me. But, then again, Mads will be pissed if I don't go. I take a deep breath and decide it doesn't hurt to give him a call, it's better to talk it out over the phone rather than an awkward text. I don't want him to think I'm asking him out or anything. Thinking of him like that makes my heart race and I immediately turn it off. I can't get hurt again.

His phone goes to voicemail and I leave a message, "Hey Nate, it's El...Elania. I have a quick question about tonight, can you call me?"

I hang up instantly questioning everything. Why did I call myself El? Why did I even call him in the first place? He's my client, he asked me to his gym, and to be polite, I accepted. But there can't be anything more. *El?* I'm such an idiot.

As I leave the restaurant, I remember that I need a new pair of sneakers; my running shoes are burnt to hell, and I'm sure as fuck not going to be embarrassed in front of Nate, or at softball.

With every light I come to, I check my phone worried I missed his call. Then I stop myself. I won't do this again, I can't put my heart out there to be jeopardized. What's it matter if he calls me or not?

Pulling into the shoe store parking lot, I take a deep breath. I have to keep myself in control. Stay focused on the task at hand. Looking in the mirror, I appear calm. I apply a thin layer of lip gloss before heading inside, doing my best to control my stressing.

As I browse the shelves of shoes looking for the right pair, my phone rings. It's him. I swallow hard. "Hey, Nate," I answer.

"Hey, El, sorry I missed you."

Christ, he called me El again. I snap out of the instant daze he puts me in, willing myself to speak. "It's all right, not a big deal at all." Then it's quiet, that horrible awkward silence that everyone hates.

"So, you had a question for me?"

"Oh yeah, sorry. I was just wondering if you wanted...I mean...what shoes should I wear? I'm shopping for them right now."

"Sneakers," he says slowly, clearly confused by my bizarre question.

"Sneakers," I repeat, staring at all of the options, wondering how I didn't have the balls to ask him to softball and let things slip away so quickly. Mads is how. Damn her for making my wheels spin about him. I was completely fine until she brought up my past and it made the present throw up in my face.

"So, I'll see you at six?" he asks.

"Yeah, six."

We hang up and I grab the first size sevens that I see, walking with my purchase to the register. I pay and toss everything onto my passenger seat, then swing by my office to check in on things.

As usual the day slips away, until I find myself checking the clock to see it's already 5:35. *Shit.* There's no way I can make it home to change, then across town to his gym. Thankfully, I have a gym bag in the back of my car. It's old as shit, from when I used to take yoga classes, but it has workout clothes in it.

Running out to my car, I open the back and dig through it. There is a pair of navy blue yoga pants, but a tank top is a totally different story. Frustrated, I pull out every last item from the bag, only coming upon some socks, another pair of pants, and two sports bras. Looking at the two bras and then down at myself, I'm fucked, I don't have a choice. I grab the purple one and some socks, then my new sneakers from the passenger seat.

I cannot believe I'm about to show up at his gym half dressed. I shake my head to myself. What choice do I have? Quickly, I change in the restroom and wish that I had time to stop and buy a shirt or tank top from somewhere.

On the drive, traffic is a bitch, in true New Jersey fashion, giving me plenty of time to get myself all obsessive and worked up. I remind myself to stay calm – I'll only be a few minutes late and I'm just working out with a friend...nothing more. As the minutes on the clock tick by, I get more and more nervous, looking down at my bare stomach.

Finally, I pull into the parking lot. It's crowded and looks super busy, making my anxiety spike that much more. But I don't have a choice. Parking in the only available spot that I see, I grab a hair tie from my center console and hop out, dragging my confidence behind me.

Walking up the stairs to the all-brick building, I check my car to make sure it's locked before entering. I'm just mentally stalling at this point because goddammit, I'm nervous. And Elania Harmon doesn't get nervous. But there's something about this man that does that to me.

CHAPTER 14

-Nate-

"What's up? You look stressed," Amanda asks me.

"You know Elania's coming to work out and…" I can't bring myself to finish the sentence. Right now I sound so dumb and insecure.

"Come on, Nate, you can tell me anything," she urges me.

"It's my leg."

"What about it?"

"She doesn't know about the prosthetic and I don't know if I should tell her now or not."

Amanda glares at me. She views my leg the same way I view her being gay. It shouldn't make a damn bit of a difference to anyone. Or change anyone's opinion of me. But it's always in the back of my mind and I fear it'll lead to rejection.

"Forgive me if I sound uncouth, but what the fuck does it matter? I mean, that's what you tell me all the time."

I look her in the eye, her sincerity shines through, I realize eventually that I'll have to tell Elania. It's just, inside my gut is telling me that the better decision is to tell her now, to not hold anything back.

"You're right."

"Damn straight I am. Now please take your ass to the locker room and change into some shorts. I'm sure she's already been wondering why you are in jeans all the time while we're pretty much trapped in Satan's ass crack all summer."

Leaning over, I give Amanda a hug. My leg or lack thereof is part of who I am. It doesn't change me as a person or hinder my abilities in any way. I shouldn't let it affect me mentally. Deep down I believe that's what led Arion to stay with Bain, but I guess that's really only speculation at this point. Maybe I'm just hiding behind it because it's easier than the full truth. Fuck if I know.

Heading into the locker room, I change into a blue pair of basketball shorts and check the time on the wall; it's 6:13. *Fuck, maybe she's not coming.* Maybe I got stressed over nothing, seeing how at this point she's almost 15 minutes late and seems to take punctuality crazy serious. So far, I haven't heard a word from her. I go back into the office and check my phone…still nothing. I'm not going to text her. If she forgot, or better yet, blew me off, then fuck her. It might actually help me out.

"Hey, Nate." Ryan, one of the girls from the front desk, comes into the office and interrupts my mindfuck.

"What's up?" I ask her, trying to hide the annoyance to my tone.

"Can I get some ones for the front register?"

"Is it out?"

"Almost," she responds. Just as I bend down to open the safe. My heart stops. There she is. Jesus Christ, there she is. Half dressed, looking hot as fuck, long brown hair pulled up on her head, showing every part of her body, and in *my* gym.

"I'll bring 'em right out," I tell her, not able to look her in the eye as mine are glued to Elania's body.

I can see she's looking for me, glancing around, fidgeting with her car key and hasn't spotted me yet.

"Okay, thanks," Ryan says and leaves the office. I do my best to not gawk over Elania, in fear that she will catch me. But it's damn near impossible. Jesus, her body is amazing. It's everything I imagined it would be under those damn dresses that she wears.

Knowing I need to get to her, I open the safe and snatch a stack of ones. Then I stand and take a deep breath. Here goes nothing. As I leave the office, with my eyes focused only on her, she is buying a tank top at the counter, and I curse myself under my breath for coming up with the idea to have custom tanks in the first place.

I pass the money to Ryan and watch in slow motion as Elania pulls her new purchase over her head. *Damn, she's sexy.* She turns and we lock eyes, both of us frozen as if it's the first time we've seen each other. Her eyes never leave mine and don't even hint at a glance towards my leg.

"Hi," she says.

"Hey," I respond, no longer gawking at her beauty. I'm respectful – I want her to feel comfortable here, with me, any time.

"Sorry I'm late," she says as I lean down to hug her and gently kiss her cheek.

"Don't be," I tell her, pulling us apart, hiding

that I'd started to stress and worry that she wasn't going to show up.

"Thanks."

"So…are you ready?"

"If you are."

I smile and place my hand on the small of her back, glancing at Amanda for a brief second. She's got the biggest smile on her face and winks at me.

"Do you want to set your stuff in the office?" I ask her.

"Yeah, that'd be great."

I direct us that way and immediately imagine closing the door and doing very bad things to her. On my desk. Against the wall. In my chair.

I change the subject in hopes that it will clear my mind. "Good choice on the shirt you bought. It's the one I designed."

"Oh really?"

"Yeah, it looks good on you."

"Thanks. This place is really nice, even better than what I saw online. Very impressive."

I take her phone, wallet, and car key, placing them in the desk drawer.

"So you looked us up online?"

"Yeah, I told you that a while ago. I was considering coming here, but the drive is just too far."

"Oh yeah. Well, don't worry, I'm gonna open something just for you."

"Just for me?" She asks smiling at me as we leave the office.

"So what's tonight gonna involve?"

Her question completely catches me off guard. My filthy mind wants to do so much with her, to her, that I've totally spaced on the fact that she's here to actually exercise. I pull myself back. I can't make her feel uncomfortable, or jeopardize our professional relationship. Right?

Fuck, she's staring at me. I'm not sure if it's because she wants me as well, or she simply wants an answer. "Let's start with some cardio," I tell her and we head upstairs to the indoor cardio track that wraps the inside of the gym.

We begin to walk and things are quiet. My head is in the gutter, and dammit, I'm not sure where hers is.

"So do you do this often?" she asks me.

I look at her blazing light eyes trying to figure out what she is asking. "What do you mean?"

"Give private lessons?"

For fuck's sake, I really need to keep my shit

together when I am with her. She makes me forget about everything else except what I want to do with her. I haven't even stressed about my leg and that's a rarity.

"Nope, I told you I don't."

"Really? I must've forgot," she asks, almost stopping us on the track.

"Yeah, I handle more of the management side of the gym and overseeing that everything runs smoothly. Lessons aren't my…" I don't bother finishing my sentence. The truth is, lessons aren't my thing. But, any time with Elania is worthwhile in my opinion. "Wanna run?"

She nods her head and we pick up our pace. We are no longer walking quickly, now both of us are moving our bodies in line together. Thankfully, my leg feels good today, so it doesn't hinder my speed at all, because Elania's idea of running is damn near marathon racing. I can tell she likes to run.

After two laps, I slow the pace. Her lungs heave in her chest and I can tell this got her warmed up enough. "Ready to lift some weights?"

She shrugs her shoulders and in this moment, I love the look of hesitation that is written all over her face. It's not something that she shows often, but it shows how real she is.

Heading to the free weights, I explain everything in detail so she knows exactly what we are going to be doing. To my surprise, she is interested and doesn't seem one bit scared.

"Why don't you try those?" I say and point to a set of dumbbells.

She looks at the ten-pound ones and tilts her head, then she steps to the right and grips the fifteen-pounders. I can see two guys watching her and instinctively it makes me jealous. Even though she's not mine, the guys don't need to gawk at her. Then she lifts the weights and looks me in the eye. Right away I forget about everything else. "How do those feel?" I ask her.

"Good."

I take one from her, the tiny bar in my hand looking so small. "Why don't you place one knee on the bench while you curl the weight for twelve reps?" I demonstrate what I want her to do and she nods her head getting into the position. The entire time my eyes are locked on the weight, making sure that it doesn't become too heavy for her.

As she begins to pump it up and down, her

form is almost perfect. Moving behind her, I straddle the bench and place my hands on her shoulders. "Up a little higher," I tell her.

She straightens her body and I watch the way her little bicep flexes and how the muscles in her back move. Christ, she's hot. Looking at her reflection in the mirror, with my body behind hers, my mind drifts. Pulling myself back to reality, we catch eyes and she stops moving. My chest is heavy, my breathing is quick, and I'm not sure what to do next.

"That was twelve," she says.

"Right. You can do the other arm now."

She smirks at me, clearly reading that I am flustered. While she does the other arm, I fully realize that asking her to work out with me was a bad idea. My cock is throbbing, and she's got to recognize what she does to me, and there is nothing I can do. After she's done, I grab a fifty-pound dumbbell to take out some of my pent up aggression.

"Excuse me," I tell her, as she sits on the bench I need to kneel on. She smiles and stands back up. I lay down fifteen reps like nothing and pray that this work out will be over quickly. My insides might explode with the tension that is now between us.

CHAPTER 15

-Elania-

"So when are we working out again?" Nate asks me.

My face is bright red. After the back and forth last night, the undercurrent obviously flowing between us, I'm not sure working out together is a good idea. I about gave into him, and for me...I can't do that. Not after what Alex did to me.

"Oh, there won't be a next time."

He smirks and holds the door open for me. I get behind the wheel of my Escalade and check the time. Today we are on schedule, which is good considering I got a call early this morning about this property that I can't wait to show Nate.

"El, there will be a next time. Don't kid yourself. So where is this place?" he asks me.

I drop the subject and stick to getting to this next house. "It's in the same neighborhood as the one you made an offer on. It's not even on the market yet so we have a good chance at getting it." I correct myself. "I mean, *you* have a good chance at getting it."

"Do you have the printout with the details?" he asks me.

"I'm sorry, I don't have anything, I literally left the house and headed straight to you."

"Elania, unprepared...I'm shocked," he teases me.

"You are such an ass. Remember I'm doing this for you."

"Just teasing, El."

His mood today seems different. He is in shorts again, like yesterday, which I take as a sign he's becoming comfortable with me and I love it. Driving together while we are both dressed so casually around town really does something to me. I just love how relaxed we both are. That professional barrier seems to have slipped, and somehow I don't mind.

He's restless in his seat though and I sense that something is bothering him, and not two seconds later, he blurts, "So are you really not gonna ask me about my leg?"

Whoa, that's way out of left field.

"What's to ask?" I question him point blank.

"Maybe what happened?"

"Nate, it's none of my business."

"True…but aren't you curious?"

I shake my head, "No, not in the slightest."

He frowns and shakes his head. Deep down, I do wonder what happened, but I read on the gym's website where it said he's a military vet, that that's how he and Nash met, so I'm assuming that's how he hurt his leg.

His knee is bouncing, clearly agitated.

"Does it bother you?" I ask him.

He looks at me and for the first time since I've met Nate, I see uncertainty on his face.

"No."

I glance at him, he's staring out the window.

"What's that matter? Spill it, Nate," I demand.

"Nothing. Really, nothing. It was dumb of me to ask you."

"No, it wasn't. I obviously can't relate to your situation, however, if I had to, I couldn't imagine the feelings and the emotions that would flood through me. I'm sure one of them would be self-consciousness. But just because you have a prosthetic leg doesn't change who you are on the inside, and yesterday, I saw what you are capable of on the outside, so please know that your leg is not a concern for me at all."

He smirks at me again and takes his hat off, running his fingers through his messy hair.

"Well, here we are," I tell him, parking in front of the condo. It looks almost identical to the last one. I grab my phone and open my email to retrieve the lockbox code. Walking up to the door, I glance at Nate and watch him looking all around with his hands in his pockets. I punch the code in and grab the key. Opening the front door, we walk inside and it is literally the same as the first place.

"I cannot believe it's actually identical!" he exclaims.

"Right? The only difference, I'd say, would be there's more natural light in here, which is not a bad thing."

I take my time showing Nate around for two reasons. This is the house for Nate and I want him to see that, but also this will be the last time that we get to do this together. However, the smile that is on his face tells me that he loves it and that is ultimately why I do what I do.

As we come back to the front door to exit, something is telling me not to leave, but Nate opens the door and I walk out, ignoring my gut. He follows and I lock up.

"So, what do you think? Are you ready to make this your home?"

He nods his head. "Yeah, definitely. I can't wait to tell my mom. She's going to be so happy."

We both get into my car and I reach for my work bag, but it's not in here. "Do you have time to stop by my office? I don't have a contract on me."

"Yeah, of course," he responds. "If you have time, maybe we could grab a bite to eat, too?"

My stomach tightens from his offer. As much as I try and fight it because of my own insecurities, I can't. All I really want to do is spend time with him.

My insides are gnawing at me. I find myself wanting to keep looking over at Nate as we drive to my office, wondering if I should tell him what I'm feeling. I've tried fighting it and it's not going away. Maybe honesty is what both of us need.

"You okay?" he asks, as if sensing my inner

turmoil.

"Yeah. Yeah, why?"

"You've gone quiet on me."

"I'm good, I promise. I'm just thinking about a lot of things and let my mind slip away." So maybe I'm not as ready for that honesty as I thought I was.

"Okay, you know I'm here if you want to talk about anything."

"Thank you, and believe me, I appreciate that. We do need to talk about your offer on this place." Chickenshit that I am, of course I deflect to the safe subjects.

We discuss the details for the condo and what he's willing to pay on the drive. Then turning into my office, I park and just before we get out, anxiety hits me full speed. Jaquelle and Alex exit, all lovey with each other.

Without even thinking, I place my hand on Nate's arm to stop him. He looks down at my hand first, then at me. "Wha…?"

But I cut him off, not letting him get any further. My lips crash hard against his, and right away, he accepts me, kissing me back.

His hand moves to the back of my head, if only to bring us closer. Leaning over the center console of my car, I hold on to his bicep, and he kisses me with so much passion that I know I am no longer controlling what I started, and I give in to him, forgetting that Alex and that whore could be watching us right now. Because being in this moment with Nate is so much more than I expected. His lips are so soft yet dominating. He knows what he wants and I like that. His scent, being this close to him, drives me mad. I'd take off all my clothes right here if he wanted me to. That's the power he has over me. It's both exhilarating and terrifying.

As he slows the kiss, I am dazed and under his spell. We rest our foreheads against each other and he rubs my bottom lip with his thumb. "What took you so long?" he asks.

I can't help but give him his trademark smirk. How do I say why I kissed him without hurting his feelings? I don't think there is a way, so it's probably going to be better left unsaid. But deep down, I'd only be bullshitting myself. I've been wrestling with my feelings for Nate, and seeing my ex just pushed me. It pushed me to make a move, a move that he clearly accepted and liked. There's no harm in that…is there?

"I could ask you the same thing."

"I didn't want to jeopardize our professional relationship."

"I respect that." Looking around, Alex and Jaquelle are gone. "Clearly, we have a lot to talk about. Let's go make an offer on your new home and then lunch?"

"Can I offer either of you any dessert?" the waitress asks us.

I shake my head and Nate answers her, "No, thanks."

"So you were gone for almost a year?" I ask him, stunned by the harrowing details of him being a POW.

"Yeah."

"I bet you were so happy to get home," I tell him.

"Not really, but that's a story for another day. My road hasn't been easy and coming home was...well, let's just say when I got the news that my fiancé had moved on and wasn't waiting for me, I almost lost my mind."

"But you didn't."

"No. On one hand, I'd been given a second chance, the gift of life...but on the other, my partner wasn't going to be there to share it all with me."

"Why would she do that?" I'm completely floored.

"She thought I was dead, like my whole family did. The military made a huge mistake and they know that. I can't really blame her."

"Were your captors ever caught?"

"I'm told they were. Their other hideout was hit hard with airstrikes, but I do still wonder if somehow they survived and are out there."

"What if they are?"

"I've kept my return very quiet. Sometimes I see people who I knew years ago and the news hadn't even gotten back to them."

I put my chin in my hands and gaze at Nate. Who knew he was such a fascinating person. I was drawn to him before, but even more so now. Then you add that kiss and I can see myself falling very fast for him. "Enough about me. Tell me about Elania."

"Oh, God, I hate talking about myself."

"Stop it. I've been dying to know more about you."

"All right, let's see…I'm from California, moved here four years ago with a guy who got a dream job and promised me the world."

"I take it that didn't happen?"

"No, it didn't. He cheated on me recently and the rest is history."

"Wow, I'm really sorry."

"It's okay. I'd rather not talk about it."

"I understand. Do you have any siblings?"

"No. It's just me. My parents both work in the school system back where I'm from."

"Which is?"

"Tulare, California. It's a small quiet town with a lot of farming, about an hour from the ocean. Great weather."

"It sounds like you miss home?"

"I do, but I miss my parents more than any-thing."

"Why don't you go back?"

"Work," I blurt out. "It's clients like you that keep me busy. I always promise my parents after this deal, I'll come home, but then there's more and more work to do. The market is just crazy right now and I love the money."

Nate's phone buzzes and he looks at it. Then places it facedown on the table. "Well, I think you need to plan a trip home. You really have to."

"You sound just the same as my mom."

"It's the truth," he says, his phone buzzes again, but this time he doesn't check it.

"You can get that if you need to," I tell him.

He smirks at me leaning back, resting his arm along the back of the booth. "It can wait. I'm completely content having a conversation with you."

We sat and talked for over an hour about everything. Our pasts, the baggage that we carry, and what we both want for the future. I've never had a guy listen to me so genuinely, to really want to know who I am. It was amazing to be so comfortable being so open and raw with him. Suddenly, kissing him didn't seem so crazy after all.

CHAPTER 16

-Nate-

"Dammit, Andrea, I told you, I can't see you any more."

"But—"

I cut her off, so frustrated that I want to hang up on her. "No buts. We're done."

She's sobbing into the receiver like we have something serious going on and asks, "Will you at least tell me why?"

"I told you a while ago that we had to stop. You want more than I can give you."

"No, Nate, I don't. I'll leave Ronnie. I just want what we have right now, nothing more."

"I can't tell you what to do, but I want you to follow your heart, and if you leave him, please do it for yourself."

"I am, I promise."

"Good."

She sobs harder and I hate that I let it get to

the point where she has become so attached to me. I never meant to let things get so out of hand.

Before we get off the phone, I have one more question for her. "Andrea?"

"Yeah?"

"You don't think he'll hurt you, do you?"

"No, he hasn't laid a finger on me in years, you know that. I'm sure he'll just shrug his shoulders. I don't mean shit to him any more, Nate."

"Okay, good luck."

We hang up and it feels good to at least know she'll be safe. It's also comforting to know that she is making this decision for herself. It can't be because she has some dream of riding off into the sunset with me. I get out of the car at my parents' house. For the first time in a long time, my dad is home. I feel like work always has him traveling.

"Hey, Dad," I call to him as he's out front working on the yard.

"How are you, son?" he asks standing and hugging me.

"I'm good. How are you?"

"I'm great. I took all of next week off from

work."

"No way, that's great." This is so long over-due.

"You're telling me. I spent the morning with your mom. It was so nice to be with her."

"I just left there myself. I had to share some news with her."

"What's that?" he asks.

"I put an offer on another place that's real close to her. I should know soon if it got accept-ed."

"That's great news. As much as I'm going to miss having you here, I know how much it means to you to have your own place, to build your own life."

"Thanks, Dad. Listen, I just stopped by to grab some clothes. I have to get to the gym."

"Sounds good. Are you having dinner with your mom and I tonight?"

"Yeah," I tell him and go through the front door. Lately, every time I come home it kills me that my mom isn't here. I wish she were. I'm so used to having her around. Now knowing she's in a rehab center, for God knows how long, is a hard pill to swallow. But, I suppress the negative thoughts and hold out hope that she will get better.

Quickly, I change my clothes. And get a text from Elania. *I'm on the phone with the realtor for the Lands End place, the sellers want another five thousand. Will you give that and possibly pay their closing costs?*

Give them whatever they want. I just want the place.

I say goodbye to my dad and make my way across town, checking my phone repeatedly, but still there is no word from Elania. My mind begins to drift, thinking back to our workout. I love how outgoing she is, and that she's willing to give anything a try. And her smile, and her laugh, and Jesus, her ass. I want to do so much more with her. Especially after that kiss. After lunch yesterday, I'm not really sure where we stand, since we didn't exactly spell it out. Obviously, she likes me, but I'm not sure I can give her what she needs. My mind is still so damaged from Arion, and I don't know if I'm ready to put myself out there again. I'd like to think I am.

My phone rings. It's her and I answer. "Please tell me you have good news."

"Of course I have good news. Did you ever doubt me?"

"No, of course not," I laugh.

"Good, well, I just called to say congratulations. You got the house and for only three thousand more."

"No way, El! Holy shit, that's awesome! You are such a miracle worker."

"No, no, no, none of that," she insists. "It's all a part of my job and why I do what I do."

"I totally owe you."

"Well, I need you to sign some more paperwork. Can I bring it to you?"

"Sure, I'm just heading to the gym."

"Great, I'll see you there soon.

I can't wait to tell my mom, so I call her first. The news almost brings her to tears. She is really happy for me, but I also know that it hurts her too, that she can't help me in the way she always dreamed of when I'd finally move out. But I hold out hope that she will get to enjoy my new home one day.

Heading into the gym, I look for Amanda, but she's nowhere to be seen. I check the calendar to see if she's working today, and sure enough, she's teaching a class. I need to talk to her about Elania and the kiss.

While I wait for her to finish, I log into the computer system and check the daily sales which look pretty damn good, then I look at the email inbox for the gym. Nothing important there. Checking the time, Amanda should be done with her class soon, and like clockwork, she comes walking into the office.

Her shoulders are slumped and she looks down. "What the fuck's wrong with you?" I ask.

"I need to get laid."

"What the fuck?" I ask her, caught off guard by this. That was *not* what I expected her to say.

She glares at me and I sense she's serious.

"I don't even want to know how that works for you. What happened?"

"Savannah's *new* girlfriend was just in my class."

"What happened to her wanting to get back together with you?"

"I don't know, I guess she found someone else." Her eyes well with tears, and it kills me to see her this upset. Pulling her close to me, I hug her tightly, as if I can make anything better. I know I can't, but I at least try.

With my chin atop her hair, I just hold her. Then walks in Elania. My senses awaken seeing her. She's in a tight blue dress, her hair is up today, and Christ, do I love it. I realize I haven't even let go of Amanda as her beauty has me immobile.

"I'm sorry to interrupt," she says a little coolly.

Amanda pulls away and looks at her. "No, you weren't interrupting."

"I just…" she trails off uncertainly and hands me the contract.

I can see the pain in her face, and I immediately realize she thinks that there is more going on than there is. Taking the paperwork from her I want to put her at ease, saying, "El, this is Amanda, my best friend, and Amanda, this is Elania."

Amanda steps to her. "It's such a pleasure to meet you. Nate has told me so much about you."

"He has?" she asks, looking at me warily.

I wink at her and she looks back at Amanda, who says, "I don't want to get in the way, and I have another training session. But Elania, it's great to finally meet you. I hope to see you around here more."

As Amanda leaves, I close the gap between Elaina and I. She's looking up at me with those eyes and those lips. There's a glint of pain laced in the crease of her brow and I don't like it. My hand finds her face, gently cradling it as a breath of air escapes her. I lean in, kissing her softly.

Right away, her lips pucker against mine. A soft whine sounds from within her. Jesus, I love how her lips feel connected to mine, how her body feels so close to me. Moving one of my hands down her body, I finally get to feel her every curve, every contour that makes her.

Finally, she slows the kiss, and as much as I hate it, it's what right. I don't need to walk out of here with a hard on.

"What was that for?" she asks as I brush her bangs out of her eyes.

"So you know there's nothing going on between Amanda and I."

"How does a kiss reassure me of that?"

"I guess it doesn't, but Amanda…" I stop myself before saying too much.

"You can tell me, Nate." I look into her eyes and know that she means it. For some reason there is something about her that is making me want to trust her.

"She's not into guys, if you get my drift."

She nods her head and I see everything click. "Oh," she says.

"I told you nothing's going on with her. But I

have to be honest with you – I do want more to go on with us." Fuck, my own words shock me. What is this chick doing to me? I can't believe I'm actually considering a relationship. That I'm not panicking even the slightest bit. That my breathing is steady and calm and not one part of me is freaking the fuck out.

She looks away from me, processing what I just said. "What does that mean exactly?"

"I'm not sure myself, but I like how you feel in my arms and how we are when we're together."

"I like it too," she whispers, both relief and tension warring on her face.

"Can we see where things go?" I ask.

"I'm not sure I'm ready. You know what Alex did to me. I can't get hurt again. It's still so fresh. So raw."

"I won't do what he did to you, I promise. I've been through hell myself. I'm not even sure I remember how to be in a relationship, but you make me want to try."

She pushes me against the wall. "Will you always be honest with me?"

I nod my head and softly kiss her lips.

"Okay, let's try."

Right away, my cock gets hard and again her lips find mine. Everything inside of me wants to close and lock the office door, to fuck her right here, but not for our first time…I won't do that.

Even though I have no plans on fucking her, I can't stop myself from grinding into her, letting her feel the full force of me. Even through our clothes, it still turns her on.

She holds on to me and we slowly stop kissing, so I move my lips to her neck where I get a very strong aroma of her scent and it drives me insane. Thank God we're not standing in front of the door. But I know that we risk someone coming in, and sometimes I do need to think with my head. Pulling my lips away from her neck in protest, I look at her through hooded lids.

"Can I see you tonight?"

She nods her head and asks, "What time are you off?" looking at me with those sexy eyes.

Fuck, NOW! "Whenever you are," I tell her, my steady voice concealing my intense desire to just say "fuck it" and get out of here.

She smiles, weaving her fingers into my hair. "Wanna meet at my place around six?"

"Six?" I grumble in protest.

"Fine, five?"

"Okay, that's better. I'd say let's go there now, but I understand that you have work." Clearly I'm not succeeding at totally playing it cool. My dick is definitely taking over.

"You do, too. Don't make me feel bad."

"I know I do. I think I even have an interview for a new trainer in about ten minutes," I suddenly remember, checking the clock, shaking off my lust-induced haze.

"I'll text you my address." She kisses me on the lips and turns to leave.

"Contract!" I blurt out. "I'll sign it, then walk you out."

Quickly I sign the papers, sliding them back into the folder and hand it back over to her. Then I grab her hand and watch as she looks down at our intertwined fingers.

With the proudest look on my face that I've had in a long time, we head outside. I sense everyone's eyes on us as we leave, and I don't give a shit.

The sun is warm and I let my eyes stare at her ass as she walks down the stairs in front of me. "I can't wait for tonight," she says, opening the door to her Escalade.

"I know, me either." And for one last time I indulge in her scent, her lips, and everything that is this amazing woman, who for some reason, likes me.

CHAPTER 17

-Elania-

What in the hell am I going to wear? I'm standing in my closet half naked and I have about a million things to do before Nate gets here. My mind has been a jumbled mess all day. But the truth is, the second his lips touch mine, everything inside of me calms. As much as I want to protect myself from heartache, I trust him. I don't know why, but being with him washes away every single fear.

My phone rings and I decide on a black dress that's been staring at me, throwing it on as I dash across my house. It's him...

I answer and the deep tone of his voice makes me feel very weak and very vulnerable, and very, very horny.

"What's your favorite food?"

"I don't have one."

"Really?" he asks.

"Yeah."

"Okay, since you prefer wine. Red or white?"

"Both," I respond, not able to make a decision in this moment to save my life.

He chuckles at my comment. "I knew I should've made these decisions myself. I'll see you soon, El."

The other end is silent before I know that he's gone. I shake my head to clear my thoughts and mentally compile my to-do list. I run around my house like a mad woman for the next hour because he'll be here soon. I feel like I'm getting nothing accomplished.

Then in an instant…it happens. I turn when there is a knock on my door. I exhale deeply, walking to it, running my fingers through my hair as I do. My stomach is a mess. I'm so nervous to have him here that I don't quite know what to do.

"Another dress," he says, scanning me up and down with his hungry eyes.

I quirk a smile up at him. "You like?"

"You have no idea. I fucking love it."

"Good. Come in."

He steps in and leans down, kissing me chastely on the lips, a swift soft movement of affection. Jesus, he smells good, wildly good. His hands are full, a brown bag in one while the other holds what must be our dinner.

"Are you hungry?"

"Starving," I tell him, walking us to the kitchen where he sets everything on the countertop. He looks so sexy in a pair of jeans and a white button down shirt. I almost begin to drool looking at him. He's got me so turned on that...

"You all right?"

"Yeah, why?" I ask confused.

"I asked you which wine you wanted," he says holding both the red and the white bottles in his hand.

"You choose."

"What's up with you all of a sudden not being able to make a decision?"

I glare at him, a tiny bit offended by his words. "I can make a decision just fine."

"Then which one is it?" he asks kissing my neck. "Red or white."

I shiver from my head to my toes, before blurting out, "Red."

"Good, El, I like that side of you. The assertive one that knows what she wants."

"Don't worry, it's still here," I reassure him,

knowing that I have to pull my head out of my ass and find my confidence again. I have to. For some God unknown reason, I've let him cloud my thoughts, and it's taken away from the strong, confident, decisive woman that I am.

"Good. Do you have a wine opener?" he asks.

I hand him one before retrieving two glasses, all the while watching his muscles as he attacks the bottle. With twist after twist after twist, his biceps are ridiculous, and when he's using them, well...kill me now, because I might faint from the sight.

He catches my eyes and just laughs at me. "You know there's more to me than my muscles," he teases.

"Oh, I know, trust me, I know."

"I haven't always been this big," he says.

"Well, I'd assume you weren't born this way," I joke.

I shake my head. "When I was held hostage, I weighed close to nothing. I was skin and bones."

"You mentioned that. I didn't think that your captors fed you four course meals and let you work out all the time."

He becomes very serious and I fear that I've said something wrong. We were just joking and I...goddamn my big mouth. "Are you okay?" I ask him.

"Yeah, I'm fine. Sorry. I just can't go back there again. It's not a happy place, or anywhere that I like to visit."

"I won't bring it up again."

"If you have questions, I always want you to be able to ask, please know that."

"Not if it's going to hurt you."

"Sometimes I just need a minute to get my head around it, that's all."

I nod my head and like that although this is hard for him, I can still ask him questions if I need to. It shows that he's thinking about me too, which was something I felt Alex never did.

He hands me a wine glass, filled to the rim, and says, "To us."

I like that. "To us," I repeat and we both swallow a bountiful drink of this delicious wine.

"Want me to show you around?" I ask him.

"Absolutely," he says and we venture off. My house isn't huge, but it's a modest size and I worked my ass off to get it. Thankfully, it all came together during a time in my life when I needed it most. Things with Alex had just fallen apart and this was my saving grace. I needed a move-in ready nest to be my safe place.

"I love your home," Nate says as we come back to the kitchen.

"Thanks," I tell him ogling him a little, too. "Wanna eat?" I ask snapping out of my fantasy.

"Sure, I brought Italian, I hope that's okay?"

"It's great. I told you, I love all food."

"You really have no favorites though?" he asks, as I pull out a few plates.

"No, I really do love everything. It sounds crazy, but I can't think of anything that I don't like."

Nate opens the to-go containers, and right away the smell invades my senses. He keeps looking at me and not just in my eyes, but he's scanning my body, like he's mentally fucking me right here.

"Do you want to eat outside or in?" I ask, trying to sound completely normal, but that look he keeps giving me is making me feel far from normal. It's making me hot, very hot, and turned on.

What Nate so easily does to my body and my mind is something that I've never experienced with anyone. It makes me hopeful that things with him could be different.

"Outside is cool with me," he says.

We make our plates, then put the extra food in the oven before heading outside. Nate somehow juggles both his plate and wine in one hand and slides the door open for me. We sit to eat, both of us locking eyes on the other. I can tell that neither of us are in the mood for our dinner. Nate's eyes keep looking me up and down. Clearly, he wants what he wants. It's one of the many qualities that I like about him, that he's not afraid to hide what he's into. Struggling to not jump into things too quickly, I make a lame attempt to start a normal conversation.

"Did I tell you I talked to the other realtor about your closing date?"

He shakes his head shoveling a huge bite of food into his mouth.

"It looks like we can close on the 13th of the month."

"Damn, that's fast. Thank you, El."

I try to stop myself from blushing when he calls me El. "Is your mom happy that you got the place?"

He nods his head taking a drink of his wine.

His strong hand wraps all the way around the glass.

"Yeah she is, but is that really what you want to talk about tonight?"

I set my fork down, knowing that I can no longer eat. My heart is pounding, rushing blood throughout my body. I really don't want to talk about work, or his house. I want to talk about why he's here and what tonight is really going to be about. But how do I do that, when I'm scared of saying the wrong things? Dating or whatever we are doing is all new to me again; I just don't know how to be.

Leaning back in my chair, I watch him eat while I sip my wine. He's content with me not answering him, and in this moment it gives me time to think. We both know why he's here. You could cut the sexual tension in the air with a knife, so I take a deep breath and follow my gut. No more talking, or thinking, or mind fucking. Automatically, my hand moves to my dress and I unbutton the top button. His eyes follow my hand, carefully watching what I am doing.

He drops his fork and wipes his face with his napkin. "Do it again," he demands.

"You first," I challenge him, but he shakes

his head and moves his hand to his pants where his very apparent cock is straining to be free. He grabs a hold of it through the rough fabric of his jeans and moves his hand. Watching him touch himself like this sparks me to move. So I obey and slowly slip the soft black fabric of each button off, until finally, I'm at the last one. I glance around, but as usual there is no one in the yards on either side of me and behind my house is open space.

"Stand up."

I do as he asks, pulling the fabric to the sides of my body so he can see me. Granted, I still have a bra and panties on, but clearly he's into what he sees. Exhaling loudly he says, "Fuck, you're amazing."

"Thank you," I respond and he gestures me to him. I comply, stopping when my thigh touches his. He licks his lips as if he wants to eat me.

"I'm going to touch you, okay?"

I nod my head in agreement. My heart pounding so hard that I'm afraid it might stop. Looking down, I watch his soft hand find my thigh. He clenches the outside and gradually moves his way up, 'til it's on my hip. I love watching him. There is a need inside of him, a hunger like nothing I've ever seen before. Sitting up in his chair, Nate takes his other hand and does the same thing. Only this time, he slides it behind me, 'til he has a firm hold on my ass.

I tilt my head back. My whole body quivers and I'm surrounded by a sense of security. It's something I haven't felt in a very long time. Looking down at him, he's so genuine and beautiful. As much as I want to rush things with him...I don't. I let Nate take the lead staying in this moment with him.

CHAPTER 18

-Nate-

With both of my hands fiercely holding Elania's flawless body, I actually think I might pass out. Everything inside of me trembles and I remind myself to take this slow. It's hard because all I want is to lay her across this table and fuck her senseless. But instead, I give her ass a small squeeze, then snake my hand into her underwear. Her eyes change a pinch and I think it's because I've caught her off guard.

Taking my time, I move my hand down 'til it rests against her sex. She barely has any hair and I like that. Automatically, I stand, looking down at her with pure, unadulterated passion. Pulling my pants down, I free my straining cock and scoot her panties to the side. She's watching everything that I'm doing, breathing so heavily that I can feel it on my chest. Taking my hard dick, I separate her hot cunt and indulge in her wetness, rubbing her so softly. We are outside in her backyard and the fact that someone could see us turns me on.

Her head falls back the instant I begin to work her. Touching her this way is heaven, my cock, her pussy. She makes the sexiest noises that I've ever heard. They are so light, but I can tell she's really into it. The sound almost brings me to my knees, but we are outside and I don't want to push things. Pulling my pants back up, I kiss her mouth and turn her body around, directing her inside.

She walks eagerly, listening to me like a good girl. I'm not sure where to take her, but thankfully she walks upstairs. I follow, still not letting go of her body. My hands are everywhere, feeling every bit of her that I can.

I want to see her; feeling her isn't enough. The second that we step into her room I pull her dress off. It hits the floor and she looks back at me with a smirk on her face. Her blue lace thong and matching bra just happen to be in my favorite color.

Grabbing my shirt, she begins to unbutton it. I hesitate for half of a second. No one has seen my scars other than my parents and doctors.

When I've been with Andrea, I've always left my shirt on. I'm worried of Elaina's reaction, and fear it could trigger a setback for me. Taking my hands, I place them over hers. She stops and looks at me. "What's the matter?" she asks.

I can't bring my eyes to hers as I answer. Self-consciousness takes over and I'm unsure how to respond to her. *Why didn't I think about this?* My breathing quickens and I close my eyes.

"Tell me, Nate," she whispers, kissing my chest through my shirt, over the spot of one of the scars. I tense. She looks up at me and I pull one of my hands away, cupping her head. She leans in to my touch, turning and kissing my palm. I close my eyes, just needing a minute to pull my shit together. My mind is racing, dragging me back to some of the moments of torture I endured, but I won't go there. I open my eyes to stay in this moment with Elania.

"I…I have a lot of scars," I exhale finishing the sentence struggling to get the words out.

"It's okay, Nate," she says so simply. "Trust me, please."

Very slowly, I drop my hands to my sides, knowing that I can't let my own insecurities ruin this time for us. Listening to her words, I let go of my fears and watch Elania continue to painstakingly unbutton my shirt. I do trust her. She knows some of what I went through, and even with just a piece of the puzzle, understands me differently that any woman I've ever known. Finishing with the last button, she looks at my body, her actions going way too slowly for the anxiety building around my lungs. My heart races, my scars don't seem to bother her as she walks around me. A sudden blast of relief hits me and her acceptance nearly buckles my knees. I was so worried for nothing.

My hands move to hers, intertwining our fingers. She stands behind me and I stay frozen. "El, you are so beautiful."

"So are you," she responds, squeezing my fingers, leaning in, kissing one of my scars. My breathing stops and I'm astounded by the rush of security this simple move brings. She pulls her hands away from mine and continues around me again moving her hand down and unzipping my pants.

I'm immobile watching her lips move all over me. She urges me to walk the few steps backwards to the bed. I comply, liking that she's taking the lead. "Sit," she orders, pulling both my pants and boxers down. My cock springs free, angry and needing attention.

She bites her bottom lip and clenches my cock, kneeling in front of me. I reach behind her and unclasp her bra. Right away it pops open, and eagerly I help her get it off. I can't wait to see her tits. Proudly, she shows them to me grabbing a handful of one, but it only lasts for half of a second, and then she engulfs me. Her warm mouth wraps so fiercely around my shaft. I grunt out, my balls instantly tightening. I've imagined her sucking me off since the moment we met.

Watching her on her knees in front of me, nearly naked, is so fucking hot. With each jerk of her hand in sync with her lips wrapped around me, she makes tiny noises as she works my shaft with her soft lips. I move one of my hands to her hair and brush it over to one shoulder. Now I can see all of her, especially her tits, so big and full, moving along with her.

She catches me by surprise, reaching down with her free hand and touching herself. She's so content, having her lips around my cock and her hand pleasing herself. But it's not enough for me. I want to work her pussy. I want to see it and feel the inside of her. I hold her face and she looks up at me.

"My turn?" I ask.

She smiles, giving me a few more strokes and kisses the head of my shaft.

"I love your mouth," I tell her as I help her stand up.

"I love your cock," she responds staring down at me. I take my pants and shoes off, but leave my prosthetic on. I want to be able to give her anything, depending on how she wants me to fuck her. "You can take it off," she says, further surprising me.

I stare at her bemused and ask, "Are you sure?"

She nods her head, saying, "Yeah, I want you to be comfortable. Your body is so sexy."

I acquiesce to her request, even though I feel uneasy removing my prosthetic. She accepts me, which is something I love. She watches me, and once I am completely naked, she steps to me. I'm sitting on the edge of the bed, her pussy right in front of my face. There is nothing separating us, except for her blue underwear, a tiny streak of wetness running down the front. She wants me.

Taking my time, I go as slow as she did and

weave my fingers into the sides of her panties. But before I pull them down, I kiss along her stomach and the inside of her thighs. She smells like heaven, a scent that at any moment could easily bring me to my knees. It's nothing that I have ever smelled before. Finally, I land one last kiss on her sex.

She whimpers, watching me slide the thin lace down her legs. Her pussy is just as gorgeous as I imagined, with a thin strip of hair and nothing else but pure soft skin. I lean right in and lick her, separating her lips with my tongue, teasing her back and forth.

I grip her leg, pulling it towards me and guide her to straddle me on top of the bed. It gives me more access to fully wrap my mouth around her as she hovers over me. She cries out in bliss and grips my hair as I relish in her taste. Her noises are a powerful combination, something different than what I'm used to. She's consistent and even, this all telling me what I'm doing is exactly what she wants.

My cock throbs, aching for attention and needing to release all the pent up anticipation that has built up from being with Elania. I don't stop my movements though – pleasing her is too much of a reward to care about myself. I'll wait, pushing her body to the edge. Holding her against my face. Then right as she begins to shudder and is about to give herself over to me, she stops and pulls away.

"What's wrong?" I ask, concerned that I did something.

"Nothing," she says and straddles my lap. Her hot cunt hovers over me. It takes every ounce of my willpower not to slam into her. "Are you okay without a condom? I'm on the pill and haven't been with anyone for months."

I agree, knowing that I only want to be with her from now on, and every time I was with Andrea we used a condom. I wouldn't bend the rules there, but with El, she could ask me to do just about anything and I would do it.

She wraps her arms around my neck, rubbing herself against me. The friction is finally too much. I need her, dammit. Reaching down, I grip myself in search of her opening. She helps me and I nuzzle right in, losing my breath, the inside of her, so warm, so flawless and tight. She starts to move slowly, keeping our bodies close. Both of us are tangled together from head to toe. Hands explore every ounce of each other's bodies. Lips leave wet kisses anywhere they can.

Fuck, she's amazing. With every shred of control I have, I fight coming so soon. Then she pushes me back and says, "I'm gonna fuck you hard, Nate." I quirk a brow at her, waiting to see what she's going to do.

Watching her above me, there's a different look in her eye, something that I haven't seen yet. Reaching up, I grab one of her tits; she pushes her breast into my hand while twisting her hair up and out of her way. Then holding it on top of her head with both of her hands, she starts to move. Only now, she's just out of my reach. But I couldn't give two shits, watching the way she rocks her body against mine, burying my dick so deep inside of her. When she moves her hips back and forth, I swear I've reached a new level of hardness.

For the first time in a long time, I am comfortable, in my mind, in my body, and I can simply relax and just *be* in the moment. Moving both of my hands behind my head, I watch her eyes follow my biceps as they flex, resting back. She picks up speed and it sets me off. Finally, she drops her hair, bracing her weight against my chest and bobbing her ass up and down, drawing out hard, long movements. I meet her thrust for thrust, moving my ass up and down, grunting as I fuck her. She likes it rough, that much is clear, so I drill her as deep as she can handle.

"Yes, Nate!" she screams.

"You like my cock?" I ask her breathlessly.

"Ahhhhhhhh, fuck. Yes. Yes," she chants and then convulses on top of me, screaming out in pleasure. Her skin turns pink and her eyes roll back in her head. I watch as long as I can. My balls are fiercely tight, screaming for their release and then on their own, without me controlling them, they let go. My body arches back and I yell, pumping my cum into her. I shiver in ecstasy, sharp, hollow breaths following the best orgasm I've ever had. I can't stop myself from moving.

Still pumping my hips, I open my eyes to the sight and feeling of her lips all over my body. Typically, one orgasm is all I need, but with Elania, I need more of her. Instantly, I flip her over and lift her body against mine, crawling us to the center of the bed. As I gently lay her back down, I begin to move and she wraps her legs around me. We stay close this time, my cock nestled deeply, her body my own paradise.

CHAPTER 19

-Elania-

"Will you stay the night?" I ask Nate apprehensively, my naked body wrapped around his and he answers right away, "Of course," calming all of my worries. Nate is different than anyone I've ever been with and for once it doesn't seem that the relationship is based on just sex. He seems to really care for me.

He holds me tighter, and my breathing has finally calmed down after we endured what was the most amazing sex ever. I've never had someone worship my body the way that he did, and having him do so was such a turn on. He cared solely about my pleasure, making me come again and again, and each time I did, he did. It's as if our bodies already know each other so well.

"You're amazing," he whispers into my hair, leaving a small kiss. My heart speeds up, slamming against my chest. I don't know where this is going with him. I'm not sure if I will end up hurt in the end, but with words like that, I'm willing to take the risk.

I remind myself to keep my guard up. He's been through a lot of shit just like I have and that makes him potentially unstable. As much as I want to trust that this is the relationship I've been looking and hoping for, I have to be careful. Pushing away all of the negative thoughts, I simply enjoy being in his arms. Christ, he's got a tight hold on me and I love it.

"What was that?" I ask, hearing a strange noise.

He looks down at me and smiles. "My stomach."

"Really?"

He nods his head. "I'm starving. I eat like a horse. I have to, to stay this big. I get hungry a lot – you'll learn that about me." Reaching down, he squeezes my ass. "I could eat this right now. It's so enticing."

I can't contain my laugh and roll over.

"What's so funny?" he asks pinning me down. I shake my head, still giggling at him. "Tell me dammit," he says tickling me.

"I've never had anyone compliment my ass before. It's small and flat. There's nothing to it."

"Nonsense; it's fucking gorgeous."

"That's sweet. Can I ask you something?"

He nods his head.

"What does 'giving us a try' mean to you?" I ask him, my pussy tight, already ready for him to work it again.

"I wanna see where this can go. I want to be your boyfriend. I want to fuck you whenever, and take you out, or keep you in, to do with you as I please. That is…if you'll have me."

"I'll have you, Nate. Just don't hurt me. I went through hell with my last break-up."

"I would never hurt you. Trust me, if anyone knows about heartache, it's me."

I smile and kiss him. We get lost for a moment and then his stomach growls again. "Come on, let me cook for you."

We get out of bed and I grab his shirt off of the floor. He scoots down and grabs his prosthetic. I can't imagine what he went through to get to where he is today. He puts it on, followed by his pants. Then I catch him looking for his shirt and I smile at him, when we connect eyes.

"I like you in my clothes," he says standing

next to me, so tall that I have to crane my neck to see his face.

"Are you ready to eat?" I ask him.

"For sure." Upon entering the kitchen, Nate sits at the bar and I open the fridge, bending over, 'cause I know he's right behind me. I push my ass towards him and remember that we have dinner in the oven. I stand up pulling it open.

"This work?" I ask.

"You said you were gonna cook for me," he grumbles.

"Fine," I complain jokingly. "I'll cook."

"No, no, no. Leftovers are fine," he says, coming into the kitchen and swatting my ass. "I'm gonna run to my car real quick."

"Do you want your shirt?" I ask.

"Nah, it's dark out."

I can't help but watch him walk away. He's limping more than usual, and his back...oh my God, his poor back. Seeing his scars in the kitchen light makes them more apparent. I shiver from the sight, feeling terrible as I imagine what he went through. But I push the thought aside, knowing he doesn't want to relive any of it now.

Turning the oven on, I reheat the food, then flip the TV on. As usual, *Extra* is on and I love me some Hollywood gossip. I listen from afar, opening another bottle of wine. Then the anchor begins to talk about Bain Adams from the Miami Heat and his wife, Arion. Oh, I love that couple. Such a tragic story how he lost his sister.

Nate comes back in with a duffle bag on his shoulder and his attention is immediately drawn to the TV. *"The happy couple are expecting baby number two early next year,"* she says and they flash a few photos of them from their recent *People* magazine shoot.

"Can you believe that? They just had a baby and now another one."

Nate's face is white as a ghost. He drops his bag and stands frozen in my living room.

"What's wrong?" I ask, instantly alarmed.

He doesn't respond to me, I walk around him as tears well in his eyes. He blinks them away as the TV show goes to a commercial. "What's wrong?" I ask again, beginning to panic.

He stumbles to the couch and flops down without speaking.

"Nate?" I ask again, frightened.

"She's my ex."

My jaw about hits the floor. What the fuck? I couldn't have heard him right, could I?

"Arion Adams?" I ask, not believing him.

"LaSalle was her last name when I knew her, but yes."

"Jesus, Nate, I had no idea."

All color has drained from his face and I fan him while we sit on the couch. I'm not sure what to say next, but I have to say something, because the look on his face is scaring me.

"I'm really sorry."

"It's okay."

"Do you want to talk about it?" I ask, settling on the fact that it might be better to just let him get things out into the open.

"What's to say? She's all that kept me alive when I was gone and when I came home, she'd moved on with that asshole NBA star. Now they're married and have a kid, and I guess another on the way."

I exhale, taking in his words. Fuck, it's a lot to process. But I totally understand where he's coming from.

"I get it, Nate, I do. Even though our situations aren't the same, I know how it feels to have the person you love choose someone else. I can't imagine how you must feel with their life being splashed across the media."

"You understand?" he asks holding on to my thigh.

"Yeah."

"I guess I shouldn't be shocked by this. I've let her go, but seeing those pictures…" he trails off.

"I'm sorry," I respond and scoot myself on top of his lap, straddling his sexy body. He holds me tightly and stares into my eyes. Our chests heave up and down, and mine just about erupts when he runs his thumb over my bottom lip.

I lean in and kiss him, wanting to wash away his pain. Wanting to make him forget about Arion and anything that has to do with her. The second our lips collide, my world stops. There's nothing else that matters in this moment except for Nate and I. His hands hold me so firmly, moving in just the slightest way, the way that makes my pussy tick.

He begins to unbutton his shirt that I'm wearing; I look down watching his hands so close to my body. Right away my insides heat in anticipation. Then the oven dings, the damn timer interrupting us. *Why do I have to be so methodical?* He throws his head back in frustration. I kiss him swiftly and hop off of his lap, strutting my ass to the kitchen before I toss him the TV remote.

"You can put on whatever you want."

"I'd rather you give me a show than watch anything on here."

I smile, preparing our food, then grab him a beer from the fridge. I glance up to see what he's put on the TV and notice light music crooning through the speakers. He's turned sideways on the sofa just staring at me.

"Are you watching me?" I ask.

"Maybe," he says and smiles. Something inside me melts, and I know I'll never get enough of that smile no matter what.

CHAPTER 20

-Nate-

"So you've moved on?" Roger asks me.

"Yeah, and this girl, she's something else."

"I can tell; this is the most excitement that I have ever seen from you. I trust that she's single."

"Absolutely. She went through a fucked up break-up with a lot of rejection and heartache."

"So you can relate, that's good. What about…Andrea?"

"I ended things with her, but she won't leave me alone. I originally told her I didn't want anything more than sex with anyone, but she's relentless. Now, I can't tell her that I've moved on with Elania 'cause that will make me sound like an ass."

"But you could. You could explain that you're not interested in a relationship with her."

"I don't want to hurt her any more than I

have. She's a sweet girl just stuck in a real shitty relationship."

"There you go again, Nathaniel, always worrying about others before yourself."

"Come on, Roger. Put yourself in my shoes."

He laughs for the first time...ever. "No, thank you. I'll stick with my wife. I'm not one to enjoy hopping around with different women."

I laugh back at him, as it was actually kinda funny. "You know what I mean. I don't want to hurt her."

"Well, you need to do something to help her accept the reality of the situation."

The timer dings, and in an unprecedented move, I'm not ready to leave. I actually enjoyed this session. "Same time next month?" he says.

I nod my head and leave his office grabbing a card with my next appointment on it. "Thanks," I tell his receptionist, noticing he did schedule me for a month from now. In recent months, I have been coming every two weeks, but I guess not anymore. Finally, good ol' Roger is seeing the progress that I am making. I shove the card into my back pocket and pull my phone out as the elevator arrives.

Of course, there are two missed phone calls

from Andrea and a text from Elania. I open the text, ignoring the calls the same way I have been recently.

Lunch? My afternoon appointment cancelled.

I text her back, **I'm having lunch with my mom, do you want to meet her?**

She doesn't respond and I wonder what's going through her mind. The elevator doors open and I head towards my car. As I begin my drive across town my phone rings, and it's her. "Hey, El," I answer, switching lanes on the freeway.

"Are you being serious?" she asks. There is a clear concern to her voice.

"Absolutely, my mom wants to meet you. Why don't we surprise her today?"

"I don't know, Nate, it's so soon."

"Who cares? Just come with me. It'll be better this way, not planning it, so you don't have a lot of time to think about things and get yourself all worked up."

The line is silent. "El?"

"I'm here. I guess…as long as you're sure she won't mind."

"She won't, trust me."

"Where should I meet you?"

"Where are you?" I ask.

"My office."

"I'll pick you up. I'm just leaving an appointment."

"Should I order any food? Since you have an extra stop now?"

"Nope, we'll grab something. I can't wait to see you."

I can hear the smile in her voice. "Me too."

"Yeah?" I ask, needing a little reassurance. I might be a guy, but we have insecurities too.

"Of course. You're all I've thought about all morning."

"Good," I tell her, feeling horny the closer and closer that I get to her office.

"Well, I should get going."

"Why?" I ask not wanting to end our conversation.

"I don't want to keep you on the phone while you're driving."

"It's hands free; talk all you want."

"Is that what you'd like?" she asks.

"I like anything that you're willing to give."

"Oh, if you only knew."

"Then come give it to me, I'm outside."

She makes the cutest noise and hangs up. I

pick my phone up and text my mom to give her a heads up. She'll be happy that I'm bringing El, so I'm not concerned at all.

I glance up, looking for Elania and can see her talking to someone through the glass windows of her office. If I had to judge, I'd say she's upset. She's shaking her head, with her hands out in front of her and walking backwards.

I unbuckle my seat belt, adrenaline alone moving me to her. But before I can get three steps, she comes storming outside. She has tears in her eyes and I hold her face. She shakes her head and pushes her way against me. I wrap her in my arms, feeling terrible to see her this upset.

"What's the matter?"

"Nothing, let's go."

"Don't bullshit me, El. What the fuck happened?" My anxiety spikes and I have to remind myself to stay calm.

"I'll tell you; can we please get in the car though?"

"Of course," I respond and kiss her lips. She leans into me, sighing heavily. As we pull away, I walk her to the passenger side of the car and look into her office. Whoever she was talking to is still staring at us. I give him a death glare. The kind that says, *I will rip your fucking head off without blinking.* He walks away; maybe my tactic worked. I close the passenger door and then walk to my side of the car. She seems a bit calmed down and is wiping her eyes clean.

"You okay?" I ask.

She nods her head. "That was my ex," she says calmly.

Really? Does she work with him? I guess I should've asked a little bit more about her past.

"Why is he at your work?"

"He's dating one of the girls there. That's why we broke up. I caught him cheating on me with her."

"Fucking asshole," I blurt out. She gives a shaky smile at my outburst.

"What did he say today?"

She turns away. "He wants to know who you are. He saw us kissing the other night out here."

"Did you tell him that it's none of his business?"

"I did, but he's a lunatic."

"Sounds like it. Do you want me to talk to him?"

"No, at this rate, I just need to find a new real estate office to work at, or branch out on my own."

"I'll support any of that. It sounds like getting far away from this asshole is what would be best. He's your ex for a reason and should leave you the fuck alone."

"Thanks," she says and grabs my hand. "Now, let's go see your mom. I've already made us late."

Happily, I start the car, loving the way her strength shines through. "Try not to stress about anything," I tell her, pulling onto the main road. "We will figure all of this out together."

She squeezes my hand and we drive in silence. I love having her with me, more so than I ever knew was possible. She's such a positive light and makes me forget about all of the bad. Even when she's going through some shit, she perseveres. After we grab lunch, we make the short trip to the facility where my mom lives.

"Should I call her Barb or Barbara or something else?" Elania asks me.

"Barb, and she might call you El – that's what I always call you when I'm talking to her about you."

"So you've talked to her about me?" she asks.

I open the back door to my car, grabbing our

lunch. "Of course I have. I told you, since day one, I've had it bad for you."

She smiles at me and wraps her arm around my waist. We walk inside the cedar, ranch-style building and are greeted right away. Then I head straight for my mom's room, feeling proud to be introducing Elania to her. "You okay?" I ask, sensing she is still a little upset from what happened at her office.

She looks down at our hands that are now intertwined and says, "I am because of this. You calm me and make everything better. Thank you for that."

I lift our hands, bringing hers to my lips. "You do the same for me. Thank *you*, El."

We walk into my mom's room and there she is. She's out of bed and one of the nurses is combing her hair. She is in her wheelchair, but not in a nightgown. She got ready to meet Elania, which makes me so proud.

"Hey, Ma," I say watching the way her face changes when our eyes connect.

"Hi, baby," she says, looking briefly at me and then locking eyes on El.

I lean down and kiss her cheek. "Ma, this is my girlfriend, Elania. Elania, this is my mom,

Barb."

"It's a pleasure to meet you, Barb," she says and shakes her hand.

My mom looks happy today. She lifts her shaky arm for a hug and I watch the two embrace. "No, Elania, it's my pleasure."

The two separate and the nurse pushes my mom to the large round table that sits by the window of her room. Elania and I pull up some chairs, and I notice my mom staring at her.

"How are you feeling today?" I ask, hoping it will distract her.

"Really good. I'm not in bed, which is a good thing."

"That makes me happy. We brought Thai, your favorite."

Elania spreads everything out on the table and I can tell that she doesn't know what to say.

"So what are you two up to today?" my mom asks, seeming to have pulled herself out of the daze that she'd been in from staring at El.

I look to Elania, letting her answer. "I'm not sure. I think I'm done with work for the day, but no big plans."

I nod my head agreeing, but there's worry in the back of my mind; I think she's done with work today because of what happened. She doesn't want to go back and deal with things and I can't blame her.

"I'm off today, saw Roger this morning, and don't have any more plans."

"That's nice. When do you close on your house?"

"In about three weeks."

"Two," Elania corrects me.

My mom chuckles at her correction. "Are you from here, Elania?" my mom asks, slowly taking a bite of food.

"No, I was born and raised in California. My parents still live there."

"What in the world brought you to New Jersey then?"

"It's a long story."

My mom glances around the room, her humor shining through a little bit. "I have all the time in the world, dear."

"A guy."

"But it didn't work out?"

She smiles and looks at me. "No, thankfully it didn't."

I place my hand on hers, "Yes, thankfully it didn't."

We continue eating, the two of them are completely lost in conversation. I sit back and watch, enjoying the connection they have. After a while, it's time for us to go and for my mom to get ready for physical therapy.

"Thanks for having us, Ma," I tell her, leaning down to hug her.

She hugs me back; there's not much strength, but I'll take anything that I can get from her. Elania hugs her too and we leave. I never linger with goodbyes or look back. They are the hardest for me. I think because when I said goodbye before being deployed, I was so sure I would return…but almost didn't. It's a fine line now as a trigger for panic attacks and flashbacks, and I don't need any setbacks. Plus, the sight of her in that chair is so heart wrenching, every single time. I can sense my anxiety lurking beneath the surface.

"Your mom is so sweet," Elania says as we pull out of the parking lot.

"She's the best. It was great to see her up today too—that's the best she's looked in months."

"Really?" she asks me, turning the music down in the car.

"Yeah, I think it's because you came. It made

her get up and care how she looked."

"Come on, Nate, she didn't do that for me."

"Of course she did."

"Well, I'm glad I had a positive impact then."

"You absolutely did."

"Do you think she is physically getting better?"

My stomach sinks at her question. "I'm not sure. I mean, she looks the best that she has in a long time, but she does seem a little slower, maybe weaker too. But it could just be me overanalyzing things."

"I don't know her, but I think she looked great. She's so sweet too."

"Thank you. What do you want to do now?" I ask, completely changing the subject, talking about my mom too much can set me back and I want to stay in a good mind frame for Elania.

"Can we just go to my place?"

"Absolutely." I put the pedal down for two reasons – she's choosing to spend the afternoon with me, and I need to be with her. We can always grab her car later because the tension between us is built up, and being with my mom wasn't the place to let my thoughts morph. Trust me, they wanted to, they might have even twisted for a moment, but I realigned myself like the good son that I am. See? I *can* be a gentleman when necessary.

CHAPTER 21

-Elania-

"Yesssssss, just like that," I scream as Nate slams into me. His hands digging into my flesh, my ass in the air, and his cock riding me so hard I can't think straight. My mind swirls with desire and pain. He hits that spot, the one where it hurts and feels good all at the same time.

Each thrust from him is matched with a grunt. I love his noises and how in the zone he is. When he gets this way, he's close...again. But so am I, even though I don't want to let go, I'll have to. Letting go means that reality will creep back in, and as much as I have been pretending what Alex did isn't bothering me, it is, and I don't want to go there now.

So I'd rather remain in this symphony that is Nate and I, our bodies so close, like they were meant for each other. His hard cock, rubbing my insides with every ridge, pleasing me so good.

I keep fighting the urge of letting go. It's self-ish, but Christ, he feels so good. Suddenly, his noises change to loud grunts – he's coming. My body ignites, letting go right with him, with no warning. Right now, there's no stopping the progression. I convulse, marveling in everything that is this man and everything that he gives me.

He slows his movements, gently stroking me, giving me every last drop of his cum. I move just a little as our bodies fall against the bed. We roll to our sides and I sigh heavily.

"Are you okay?" he asks.

I look in his eyes and find strength. Nodding my head to tell him that I am… although…I'm not sure if I really am okay.

"Have you thought anymore about what I offered?" Nate asks.

I chuckle a little. "I appreciate you trying to help, I really do. But if you tried to talk to Alex, it wouldn't do a damn thing."

"Then why don't you talk to him?" I cringe at the thought. It's bad enough seeing him and Jaquelle together, much less having to talk to him.

"You saw how upset he makes me. I'd rather

take my chances and hope he leaves me alone. Thankfully, most of what I do, I can do from home."

"Come on, El, listen to yourself. Do you really want that? You have to do something. Don't let this prick have this control over you. Avoiding it and hoping he will go away isn't going to solve anything."

I toss my head back in frustration. What can I really do? "Let me think about it. Right now I gotta eat; I'm starving."

He kisses me and says, "Good. Me too. Do you wanna go grab something?"

"If you want to."

"I just want to make you smile," he says sitting up in bed.

"You do. I'm sorry if this has my head twisted. You make me so happy. Being with you right now is the only thing that's keeping me sane."

He laughs at my comment. "Now, that's a first. Wait 'til I tell my psychologist that."

"You have a psychologist?" I blurt out, immediately feeling like an asshole for sounding so pompous.

"I do. It's required by the military that I see him."

"Sorry, I didn't mean to say it that way."

"It's okay," he says getting dressed.

"Do you see him often?" I ask.

He nods his head pulling his shirt over it. "He's helped me through a lot of shit, especially with my PTSD and all that."

I follow suit, not really sure how to respond to him. "I've never talked to anyone."

"You should, Roger would be happy to help you. Especially with all this shit that happened with your ex. He'd give you a clear perspective on how to handle things.

"Maybe," I respond, scared to commit to anything at the moment. "Where should we go eat?" I ask hoping that getting out of the house will help me.

"I think I have the perfect place. Do you have a blanket we could bring?"

"Yeah." I rip the comforter off of my bed and he laughs.

"That'll work. Dress warm."

I put on some sweats and a hoody then turn to him. He's sitting on the edge of the bed watching me. "You're so gorgeous, you know that?"

I wrap my arms around his neck and look

into his brown eyes. They're so dark that they sparkle. And when he looks at me, I love the way they dance.

"So are you," I respond and kiss him.

He kisses me back. The instant our lips touch, all my worries vanish. All that matters is Nate and I.

"Let's get going," he says once we stop, with a huge grin on his face. I brush the hair out of my face and grab my comforter. "On second thought, do you have something smaller?" he asks.

Leaving the comforter on my bed, I grab a soft throw from the hall closet. Then we load up in Nate's car and hit the road. As we drive, I try and decipher where we are going based on each turn he makes. I'm surprised when he pulls into the local supermarket.

"You wanted food, right?"

"Of course, but I have food at my house."

"Just follow my lead here, I don't wanna ruin the surprise."

"Okay." We get out of the car and head inside. Nate grabs a small handheld basket and I grab his other arm, holding it as we go through the store. Shopping with Nate is fun; I could definitely see us doing it more. Once we check out, we load up and head to our final destination.

"Can I at least have a hint?" I whine.

"I gave you one."

"Saying we are going to eat this food there doesn't count. I want to know where we are going."

"Can't help there."

"Please?"

"Be patient," he says reaching over, running his right hand up my thigh and then finally clenching my pussy. He cups it and holds me, completely content. I sit back, obeying his word. He wants patience, I can give it to him. I watch Nate drive, so in control, the darkness of the night making his skin glow. Every time a car passes us by there is a glimmer in eyes. Looking at Nate makes me lose track of where we are going. "Why are you staring?" he asks rubbing over my sex.

"I'm focusing on patience, like you asked."

"Good, then stare away."

He keeps driving, taking turn after turn after turn, and I wonder at this point if he's just driving in circles. But it doesn't matter, I'm with Nate and that makes me happy.

Finally he turns down a familiar road. Along-side of us is the Atlantic. I wonder if we are going to have a picnic on the beach. Blanket, food, beach…that has to be it.

"I know where we're going," I tell him.

"You do?" he asks, glancing at me.

"The beach?"

He shakes his head. "Nope, not the beach."

"Really?" I was positive of it.

The road suddenly forks off and Nate goes to the right where there is a desolate little lot. He pulls in and nudges the nose of his car up to the edge of the cliff. Looking out the windshield, the expansive ocean lies before us. It is dark, but the moon shines down casting just the right amount of shadows that show peaks of waves here and there. Jesus, the waves are huge tonight.

"Let's get out," he says.

I obey, walking to the front of his car. This view is absolutely breathtaking. Nate sets the blanket and food on the hood, then comes to me. We stand together, his arms around me, chin atop my shoulder, and his sweet breath dancing on my skin.

"It's high tide," he says.

"It's amazing."

"I'm glad you like it."

"I do. Do you come here often?"

"I actually haven't been here before. It's turtle egg laying season, I read about it online. Apparently there are a ton of turtles that were born on this exact beach and come back every year to lay their eggs. I'm surprised there aren't more people here."

"Me too, but I like that it's just us."

He kisses my neck then lets go of me. We get everything all spread out on the hood of his car and take a seat. I keep my eyes on the beach looking for any turtles. Nate's phone rings, I glance at him as he pulls it out of his pocket. Right away he ignores the phone call and then smiles at me.

"Sorry about that."

"Don't be."

"Are you ready to talk about this whole work situation again?"

"Not really," I respond completely honest. I don't want to talk about it tonight. Anything that has to do with Alex gives me anxiety.

"I've been thinking about something; just hear me out, okay?"

I nod my head, not sure of what he's going to

say, but I trust him.

"Well, you know I want to open a second Mechanical location and I think I found a place."

I glare at him – how did he find a spot without me?

"Don't worry, I'm not working with another realtor, I just happened to drive by it. I stopped and looked in the windows. It's an industrial building off of route seven with a strip mall attached."

"I've heard of it, Nate. That property has been on the market for almost a year."

"I talked to one of the tenants and that's why I think I could get it, and at a good price. Then you could have an office in the strip mall and work on your own, and we'll either rent or sell the other spaces."

I'm a little shocked by his offer. Plus, hearing him say "we'll" regarding something so huge just…throws me off. "Wow, Nate, thank you. It all sounds great and is really generous, but I'm just not sure that I'm ready to venture out on my own though." And committing to something with him this big is a huge step that I'm not sure I'm ready to make.

"Why not?"

"I don't know."

"Talk to me, El. You can tell me anything."

"I don't want to move in too soon and then start to spend too much time together."

He rolls his eyes at me. "Come on, that's the last thing you should be thinking. We'll be doing our own things while we are at work."

"I also don't want to do this and end up being a flop having to walk back in there with my tail between my legs."

"It's scary, I get that. Trust me, I knew nothing about running a gym when we started Mechanical, but I learned, and I'll help you get things started too. Please don't worry about us though, this is gonna be good for us," he says, handing me a fresh beer.

"How am I gonna get clients to even come into the door of my office?"

"Well, I'm sure you already have word of mouth on your side from everyone that you've helped. Plus, there are so many other ways that we can market you."

My stomach is in knots. I don't want to hurt Nate's feelings, but I don't know if I'm ready to do this. What Alex did to me was terrible and I never want to endure anything remotely similar to that again. But can I trust Nate? One side of me says I can, but something else is telling me to keep my guard up.

On the other hand, I have always dreamed of having my own agency, and with Nate's help, I think we can make it happen. I realize, it's a risk after all. But what's life if I don't take risks? Yes, everything that we are and know is so new. But something inside is telling me to follow my heart and to just do it. Nate is not Alex and I have to trust that he won't hurt me the way that Alex did.

"You promise you'll help me every step of the way?" I ask with a shaky voice. I have no reason to not trust Nate so I'm going with my gut. I can't believe that I'm about to agree to this.

"I promise," he says, wrapping a tight arm around me.

I trust in his word more than I have anyone's in my entire life. It's a scary thing to do, but for once, I do. Looking into his eyes, they tell me that he wouldn't let me down. There's something comforting about Nate, something so reassuring. I think it's his past, that we both have known the deep pain of heartbreak, of being thrown over for another by the one we've loved, that makes me trust him. And for once in a relationship, it seems that he's been so open and honest with me, sharing such deep secrets and experiences. So I'm following my heart with this one and from now on, I'm putting my trust in him and moving forward.

CHAPTER 22

-Nate-

It's loud, but the atmosphere is good. Drinks are flowing through everyone and I love being out with El. Watching her on the dance floor, she's got the biggest smile on her face, and now that we have a plan to execute together for the future, it helps both of us so much.

Nash is watching Jess like a hawk, and when the girls step away to the restroom, I take the opportunity to talk to him about the second location for the gym. Especially because he's leaving town for her birthday. "I think I found a spot to open Mechanical 2."

"Really?" he asks.

"Yeah," I grab my phone, pulling up the listing pictures and slide it in front of him.

He scrolls through, not really saying much. Then asks, "How much?"

"Just a little under a million. If you like it, I'll

try and get it. There's potential for additional income with the strip mall. There are still a few open stores in there paying rent now."

"Nate, I think it would be dope, but I want us to make the right financial move."

"I promise, we will. Have I let you down at all?"

He shakes his head and raises his beer to me, and I do the same. "To Mechanical 2?" he asks.

"Hell yeah."

"What are you two celebrating?" Amanda asks as she sits down next to me.

"The possible new home of our expanding empire. Behold: Mechanical number two." I pass her my phone with the pictures and she looks through them intently.

"Damn, that place is huge," she says.

"It would be perfect. I'm gonna see if I can make an offer and close the deal quick, with Elania's help of course."

"Speaking of, where is she?" Amanda asks.

Just then she comes out of the restroom, both her and Jess are giggling walking arm and arm. Clearly, they've made a connection.

I don't have to answer Amanda. She sees the two girls coming towards us and her eyes are just as fixated on them as are mine. "Hi, Amanda," El says, giving her a hug.

Jess says hi as well and then drags Nash onto the dance floor. As the three of us begin to talk, my phone rings. It's sitting in the middle of the table, right where Amanda set it down, face up for the world to see. As it rings, Andrea's name shines on the screen with a picture of her basically naked. *Shit, I forgot to delete her contact.* I grab it, trying to hide it, but not quickly enough. Elania's eyes were glued to the screen.

She's still staring at the table, right in the spot where my phone had sat and won't look at me. I decline the call, watching her, waiting for her reaction. *What the fuck do I say?* She finally looks at me and asks, "Who was that?"

"No one, El. It was no one."

Tears fill her eyes and I catch Amanda slip away out of the corner of my eye.

"Don't bullshit me, Nate, I'm not fucking stupid. Who was that? She's fucking naked."

"She's no one, I promise, El."

She glares at me, tears running down her cheeks when she blinks and I hate that this is happening.

"You're really going to lie to me?"

"I'm not lying," I say, reaching for her arm. She pulls away from me with disgust written all over her face. Just the gesture alone is hurtful enough, but the look in her eyes absolutely kills me. "Please, El."

"Don't '*Please, El*' me, I gave you the fucking chance to tell me who she was and you won't." Angrily, she grabs her purse off of the chair and leaves.

I react right away, following her outside. No! She can't drive – she's been drinking – plus, I can't let her walk away from me. I need her. Her legs move quickly, and the second we step outside, I grab her, spinning her around and force her to look me in the eye. I have to tell her the truth about who Andrea is. She's not going to let this go until I do.

"She's someone I used to sleep with, before you. But that's it. I never dated her and I haven't been with her since we've been together.

She looks at the ground and then asks, "I thought Arion was the last person you were with?"

I shake my head, disgusted for being dishonest.

"Then why not tell me that in the beginning?"

"I don't know, I didn't think…I guess."

"I guess?" she repeats and laughs, starting to walk away from me.

I step in front of her. My leg gets wobbly as I move, but I don't care, I have to stop her.

"She means nothing to me, she never has. Please know that."

"Well, you slept with her, she had to mean something, and why is she calling you anyways?"

"She's having a hard time letting go, she wants more from me. I told her that I'm not interested and have been ignoring her, but it's not helping."

She wipes her tears away with the back of her hand and shakes her head. I grab her body, hugging her tightly against my chest and kiss the top of her hair. She stands there for a few seconds with her arms down and it worries me. Then she clings to me, crying.

I wrap my arms around her back, welcoming the closeness. Welcoming the fact that she's not running from me. I can't lose her – period! In the short time that I've known her, she means more to me than I ever imagined. She might mean as much to me as Arion did, and that was something I never dreamed would happen.

I'm afraid to move or say anything. I'm really pissed at myself for not handling the Andrea situation better when I was still seeing her. I should have never let things progress with her. I knew it was wrong all along, but I'd been thinking with my dick and not my head. My head just couldn't handle anything.

And now here I am trying to clean up things with El. We stand frozen, she is tucked so comfortably in my arms that I hope for us to move past this, for her to know that she's all that matters to me.

"I'm sorry, Andrea," I tell her, only making the tears run more.

"I don't understand, I thought we had a connection," she says between labored breaths.

I hate to be honest with her, but maybe that's the only way to get through to her. She's acting like I led her to believe we had a future when all we ever did was fuck. She's been sitting in my car for almost fifteen minutes and we've done nothing but go over the same things.

"Andrea, sexually we did. But for me it wasn't for the right reasons. You remind me so much of my ex that when we started to hook up it was just to fill that void. I know it wasn't the right thing to do and I apologize for that. But I was a mess when we met and when I look at you, I see her. You deserve to be wanted for *you*. And that's not healthy for me. I need to move past that part of my life. I need a fresh start."

"We can have a fresh start together," she says grabbing my hands. "I'm your type. I can give you everything that you need." I pull one of mine away and pat the top of hers. "No, you can't. I've moved on," I finally tell her, fed up with her fucking persistence.

She looks a little stunned and I do feel terrible for hurting her. I really do, but it has to be done. I didn't want to tell her about El, or even bring her into this, but I can't have her continue to blow my phone up the way that she has.

"You moved on?" she asks.

"Yeah."

"When?"

"A while ago." I smile just thinking of El.

Andrea nods her head as if she finally gets it.

"I had no idea. I'm sorry."

"It's okay. I truly want nothing but the best for you. Maybe you and Ronnie could make things work?"

"I doubt that."

"Why?" I ask curiously.

"I told him about you."

"You did—"

My sentence is cut off by a baseball bat smashing through my window. "Shit, that's him!" Andrea screams. I start my car and pull out of the parking spot. He hits it again just as I peel off.

"What the fuck?"

"Oh my God, Nate."

"How the fuck does he know where you are?"

"I don't know."

"Dammit," I scream, looking at my window, so pissed at the situation. "Did you tell him you were gonna see me?"

"No."

I keep driving, my internal wheels spinning. I always thought one day I'd come face to face with the douchebag, but I never thought that it would be in these circumstances. Looking over at

Andrea, she looks fucking scared and I trust that she didn't tell him, as she says. The crazy fucker must've followed her.

CHAPTER 23

-Elania-

I soak down deeper into the warm water of my bathtub and just want to scream. My insides are a mess. Part of me believes Nate; that he has nothing to do with this girl anymore. But the other part of me, the part that is nagging in the back of my head, is telling me that he's lying. That trusting him is a mistake.

Why else would he have been coming on to me so strongly and making all these huge plans, like wanting me to leave my job? Unless it was a cover up for his lies, to make me think he was more into me than he is, so he could have the best of both worlds. Me and her.

I take a gulp of wine and dry my hand to decline his incoming phone call. I just need some time alone tonight. I need to process everything and figure out what my heart really wants. I told him everything was fine, but then the more time I've had to think about things and the more anxious that he seems, I just feel like something isn't adding up.

He calls me again and this time I sink down into the water, keeping my eyes tightly shut, but…I open my mouth and scream as loud as I can. I need a release. It's therapeutic. There's something about letting everything inside of you out, that's so…calming. Slowly I slide up for air, hoping for clarity and the answers, but instead I come up with heavy breaths and my phone is still ringing. I can't avoid Nate forever; he's relentless. For now though, I'm holding out.

I take another drink of wine and decide to get out of the tub. I've had far too many glasses and am starting to get light-headed, plus the heat of the water isn't helping the situation at all. As I stand and dry myself, I do wish Nate was here. I love the way he watches me. So intently and interested in everything that I am doing, but it's also a shame that he broke my trust. It was so fucking fragile to begin with.

As the depth of the situation that we are in swirls in my head, I wonder if anything that we have is real. For all I know, he *is* seeing that girl too and he's been with her all along. I pray that he isn't. I don't want to think that he would just string me along. But…maybe he would. What do I really know about him anyways?

After all, I didn't even know about her. I thought that the last person he had been with was Arion. The wine is settling in and my body is so relaxed. I let my towel drop to the floor and get into my bed. As confusing as everything has been, I still miss Nate, his arms around me, his soft lips on my skin, and the noises he makes as he falls asleep…

Suddenly, I wake to loud banging and the faint sound of my name. I'm disoriented and it takes me a minute to pull my thoughts together. The banging continues and I realize that it's my front door. Getting up, I grab my towel from the floor and stumble to answer it.

Glancing out the peephole, it's Nate. Instinctively, I open the door. He looks exhausted, but so sexy.

"What the fuck, El?" he questions me, barging inside and closing the door behind him. "I've been calling you for hours. Thank God you're all right."

"I'm sorry," I clear my throat. "I fell asleep

after a bath and didn't hear my phone."

"Is everything okay?" he asks, clearly worried.

I nod my head and walk to my couch. I'm not about to get into the details of the mindfuck that I've been living.

He sits next to me, making sure that we are touching. "I've been so worried about you."

"I didn't mean to worry you."

"I'm just glad you're okay," he says pulling my body against his. I give right in, nuzzling as close to him as I can. He smells breathtaking; his scent calms me giving me a sense of comfort. *Could* he really be lying to me?

"Listen, I need to tell you something."

I nod my head, already sick to my stomach. What in the world could he need to tell me now?

"I saw Andrea today."

Right away, anger consumes me. *He did what?* Sensing that I'm pissed, he cups my cheeks. I try and pull away but he holds me close to him. "Hear me out. I told her she has to stop contacting me. I've told her before, but this time I made it clear."

Pushing his hands away, I get up and walk away from him. He fucking lied to me – again.

"What's the matter, El?"

"Are you that fucking dumb?" I ask keeping my distance.

"Come on, I'm trying to be honest with you."

"Are you?" Rage pulses through my head. I'm in a daze; this is just like the situation I was in with Alex all over again and I hate myself for letting things get here.

"Of course I am."

"Nate. If you were, then you would have told me before you saw her."

He looks down at the ground and barely nods his head. He knows I am right. I really don't care what he told her, I just can't believe he's up and seen her again, regardless of the supposed reason.

"You should've told me. Maybe I would have wanted to confront this girl with you. To get the point across."

"Would you?" he asks in a somber tone.

"Of course I would. But you didn't give me that chance."

"It's better you didn't," he whispers under his breath.

"Excuse me?" Irritation has the best of me

right now. I never knew that Nate could piss me off so badly. Before he can answer, fury takes over and wants him out. "Nate, you need to leave!" I shout.

"What? No!" he yells in return.

"Yes, you're being an asshole."

"Baby, I'm not trying to." He walks to me and I back step doing my best to hold my towel up 'til I am against the wall. "Please don't be this way. Let me explain things, okay?"

"You did."

"Stop!" he says, pressing his lips against my neck. I freeze, my senses heightened. "Just listen to me. Don't run or fight me, please?" he begs. His eyes are as genuine as ever. I reluctantly stop fighting him and he takes my hand, walking me back to the couch.

"She has a boyfriend and he found out about her and I."

He pauses and stares at a lone string on my towel. Twisting it between his fingers.

"Did you know she had a boyfriend?" I ask. He nods his head. "Fuck, Nate." I'm so pissed off, I can't even believe that he did that. I'm done.

"I'm sorry, El. Please calm down."

"Are you kidding me? I can't stay calm, Nate. You helped her cheat." My head is about to explode. Who is this man? Is anything that he has ever told me the truth? Suddenly, I feel like I don't know him at all.

"It was wrong of me, but he's an asshole. He doesn't care about her."

"Nate, that doesn't make it right. I went through that shit with Alex, and it's the worst feeling in the world. It's a horrible thing to do to another person and you condoned it. Think about how he feels, finding out what she'd been doing."

"I know, but this guy is clearly off his fucking rocker. He found out where she met me today and smashed my car with a fucking baseball bat. That's why I said I was glad you weren't there. It kept you safe."

My heart drops. He did what? What kind of Jerry Springer shitstorm did I just stumble right in the middle of? I knew from the beginning that being with Nate was a risk. But I never imagined this.

"Talk to me, El. What are you thinking?"

"I'm just confused. Who *are* you?"

"You know who I am. Everything I've ever

told you is the truth. I ended things with her before you and I got together. You've changed me. You make me feel."

"I have a hard time believing that."

He shakes his head and grabs my hand. "Please don't doubt me, or what I feel for you." Taking my hand in his, he places it over his chest. His heart beats profoundly, it's so strong. His eyes are pleading for me to forgive him.

"See this, that's not a lie. It's the truth and how I feel for you, so strongly that I can't control it."

"What are you gonna do going forward?" I ask, wondering if he has a plan.

"I'm going to do everything I can so you know that you mean the world to me."

A small smile breaks out, and I say, "No, I mean about this girl and her boyfriend."

"Well, I told her about you, so I have a feeling she'll respect that and really leave me alone this time. Regarding her boyfriend, I'm hoping that today he only followed her there and this will be the end of it, now that he's gotten his payback."

"What if it isn't?"

"I'd rather not go there."

"But you have to. You don't know who this guy is or what he's capable of."

I let out a deep breath that seems I've been holding forever. I can't believe that this happened. Everything that I thought I knew about him I am now questioning. Looking into his dark eyes, what I once was so sure of, now I don't know at all.

"Are we gonna be okay?" he asks.

I shrug my shoulders. "I don't know, Nate, you tell me."

CHAPTER 24

-Nate-

I sign the receipt for the new window that was just installed in my car and hope this is the last of the Andrea debacle. I filed a police report earlier today and want nothing more than to focus on the future with Elania. I've now been one hundred percent honest with her and want us to get back to that really good place we were at. I hate myself for doing this to us. Just when her walls were coming down, I ruined it all. But she seems to be moving past it, letting me rebuild her trust, even though I really don't deserve it.

The guy hands me my copy of the receipt and I thank him, then look over his work as he gets in his van. It looks damn good to me. I toss the receipt in my car and pull my phone out right as it begins to ring. It's Elania.

"Hey, baby," I answer, leaning on the bumper of my car, wanting to do everything right going forward.

"I like it when you call me that," she says.

"I know."

She giggles before proceeding; she's in a really good mood today. "So I got a hold of the selling agent regarding the property for Mechanical 2."

That's why – business makes her happy.

"And?" I ask, basically cutting her off.

"Well, he's serious about selling and since you guys are paying in cash, he's willing to make a deal on price and everything you've asked for."

"Let's make a deal, babe."

"That's what I told him. Well, not exactly, but you get my point. Could I swing by the gym and go over this with you and Nash?"

"Nash is out of town, so I can come to your office," I tease, knowing that she is working from home today.

"Nate!"

"What?"

"I'll come to you, see you soon," she says and hangs up.

I smirk and head inside. The gym is pretty slow today, but that's normal for a weekday at ten in the morning. I check in with the new guy working the counter before heading back into the office.

Signing back into the computer system, I notice an email from my dad. It's been so long since I've talked to him, but I've been so consumed with Elania and my mom and he works all the time.

To: Nate Wilcox
From: Jeffrey Wilcox
June 5, 2015 9:53am

Hello Nate,

I apologize for the email, rather than calling, but I'm currently on a flight. I wanted to talk to you about your mom's birthday. She doesn't know this yet, but I've arranged for her to have a weekend at home. There will be a nurse there 24/7 and I thought she would really enjoy spending some time away from the facility with her friends and family. With all that said, would you be willing to pick her up this Friday and bring her home?

Dad

A smile comes right to my face. My mom is

going to be ecstatic to be going home for the weekend. As I begin to email my dad back, warm hands shroud my shoulders, slowly moving their way up my neck.

I growl out of instinct, leaning into Elania's touch. Damn, she was fast. She leans down kissing me on the cheek and whispers, "I've missed you today."

I turn in my chair, pulling her onto my lap. "Then you should have let me come to you."

She smiles at my remark acting innocent. "I was in the area." I love it when she acts like this, so shy yet confident, all mixed up into one, but deep down her pussy is wet and she wants me to fuck her. I spin us away from the door, sliding my hand under her dress. The only thing separating us, is her lace panties. Ever so gently I brush them aside and begin to rub her clit.

"You were saying?" I ask, watching how her face changes. A sheen of sweat gradually covers her from head to toe and I know now that she won't be able to make a comprehensible sentence.

She kisses me and I lean us back, taking my free hand and controlling her head. She tightens her legs around my hand and it drives me mad when she holds me this way. I should stop. If I don't gain some self-control in the next few seconds, then this won't end, and this is *not* the place to fuck. I mean…I'd do it, don't get me wrong, but I'd rather be able to take my time with her and not worry about someone catching us.

Pulling away, she throws her head back. I rest my hand on the side of her thigh and kiss her neck. "Do we have to stop?" she asks.

I nod my head, "Trust me…I don't want to." She exhales and gets off my lap. "You don't need to get up."

"Oh, but I do, Nate." She pulls out her iPad from her purse. "The seller emailed me some stipulations in writing. I told him I'd present them to you guys." I can see her switch into professional mode right away and it turns me on. My cock twitches in my shorts and I want to fuck her. I should close the door right now, and handle her on my desk. She opens the email and begins to spout off a bunch of shit. I roll my chair over to the door and kick it closed. She looks at me and raises an eyebrow.

"It was getting loud, sorry," I tell her.

She keeps reading and I grip my cock

through my shorts, stroking it vigorously. Goddamn, this woman is fucking killing me. Finally she stops and pulls her eyes away from the iPad. "What do you think?"

She glances down and sees me pleasing myself. Her cheeks flush and she almost drops her iPad. I take it from her and set it on the desk.

Without a word she steps to me, licking her lips, and I grab her thigh rubbing my hand up and down. "On your knees," I order and within half of a second she drops to the ground.

I scoot to the edge of the chair, watching this gorgeous woman that is all mine take me over. Her dark hair hangs on my legs, so I brush it over to one side giving me a full view of that sweet mouth as she engulfs my dick from top to bottom. She swallows me, swirling her tongue along the way.

I grab her hair and move my hand along with her. Pushing her mouth a little more each time. Her eyes are closed and she takes one of her hands bringing it underneath her dress. My balls instantly tighten at the thought of her pleasing herself. She moans and I do my best to control myself, but her lips are so fucking tight. I feel like I'm in high school again as I let go. All reality, thoughts, and worries are washed away as I cum in her sweet mouth, which she happily accepts.

"Are you sure everything's okay?" I ask Amanda before leaving the gym for the day. She's been really quiet and just not herself. I even asked her to work out with me and she said no.

"Yeah, I'm good," she says, taking her eyes away from mine and looking around the gym. "I just..."

"Don't bullshit me. What's up?"

"I'm...I'm seeing someone."

What the fuck? "Why didn't I know this?"

"I wanted to tell you, but I'm really nervous for you to meet her."

"Why?" I ask, pissed that she never told me.

"'Cause, I really like her."

"Who are you and where is the girl I used to know? You don't keep things from me."

"I'm sorry," she says.

"Who is she?"

"She's someone that comes to my classes. I guess we clicked and things have moved really quickly."

"Well, thanks for telling me now," I grumble grabbing my gym bag and car key. Leaning in, I kiss her cheek.

"I want you to meet her."

"Okay, just text me and let me know when."

I leave kinda pissed, pissed that Amanda didn't tell me that she was dating anyone. Not that it's any of my business, but I tell her everything, and besides I've seen her get hurt time and time again. When it happens, it kills me. I don't want that for her. I want her to be happy like I am. I guess I should have known something was up when she's become distant lately. It wasn't just my relationship with Elania that's put a gap between us. It's her seeing someone new.

Pulling into Elania's driveway, I can't wait to just relax tonight. Getting out of the car, I take a deep breath of air into my lungs and walk inside. The music is loud and El is in the kitchen trying to open a bottle of wine. She doesn't see me and I just watch her for a few moments. Her hair is up in a messy mound on top of her head. She's wearing a tight pair of yoga pants and a tank top. I can't let her struggle anymore. Quietly, I set my stuff down and walk to her. Wrapping my hands over hers. She jumps out of her skin and I laugh lightly at her.

"Dammit, Nate, you're early."

"Am I now?" I ask kissing her lips. "I must have lost track of time after you sucked me off today."

She giggles and hands me the wine. "I can't find my other opener."

I open it and say, "I got it. I must not be that early, unless you're drinking without me."

"After the day I've had I could use a glass."

"What happened?" I ask, concerned that she had a bad day.

"Veronica called today, asking when I was coming back and I told her I wasn't. So she wants me to clean out my office by the end of the week so they can get someone else in there."

"Isn't that a bit fast?"

"I guess, but she needs to fill the space."

Tears fill her eyes and I grab her face, holding her cheeks in the palms of my hands. "Don't cry, baby, I'll take care of it."

"How?" she snaps.

"I'll have movers go in and pack up your stuff."

"No, Nate, I can handle it."

"But I want to. Let me do this for you. Then you can let that place and everything that goes along with it go. You're doing great on your own and you won't be working from home for long, we'll get you an office."

She gives me a little nod. "Well, I do have some good news. I just got off the phone with the seller for Mechanical 2 and we have a deal."

"No shit," I blurt out, grabbing her and basically lifting her in the air.

She hugs me and I can't wait for this, for both of us. It's going to be great to be working next to each other every day.

"So, he agreed to everything?" I ask.

"Everything," she repeats.

"I have to call Nash."

He's gonna be so stoked. We have come so far in this business. When we opened Mechanical, we just dreamed that it would stay afloat. Now to be making good cash flow and on the path for our second spot is unreal.

CHAPTER 25

-Elania-

Looking in the mirror, I am a nervous wreck. Today, I'm going to meet most of Nate's family. It's his mom's birthday weekend and I don't want to let him down, but at the same time, I am really worried to meet everyone.

"Damn, you are hot," he says drying himself off from the shower.

I glance at his sculpted body and just shake my head. "What?" he asks, putting on his prosthetic.

"You're the one to talk about being sexy. Have you seen yourself lately?"

He stands up and flexes his chest muscles at me. "I do look good, huh?"

I laugh and head into my closet, calling out "And you're so humble."

He laughs. "So you're driving with me,

right?" he asks.

I place my hand on the wall and balance as I put on one of my heels.

"El?"

"I don't want to intrude, Nate. I told you that."

"You're not intruding. My mom loves you."

"But she thinks she's going to an appointment, won't it be weird if I am there?" I ask coming back into my room. He's buttoning the last button on his white linen shirt and I almost die. Swallowing hard, I keep my focus on the conversation at hand.

"Absolutely not. I asked her. Plus, she's doing way better than she was when you last saw her. That's the only reason that I get to drive her."

"Okay," I agree as he pulls my body close to his.

"It'll be great. For Christ sakes, she'll be happy to have you to distract her, she thinks she's going to the hospital for more tests. Imagine how excited she's going to be when I take her home."

"Okay, let's get going then," I tell him.

"Absolutely, sexy, but do you have a pen first?"

I look at him strangely. What in the world does he need a pen for? I hand one to him and he pulls a card out of his bag and signs it. "Here, will you sign it too?"

"Nate..." I complain, feeling bad.

"El, you gave me the idea to buy her the new Kindle. Just write something and sign your damn name."

I snatch the pen from him knowing that he won't take no for an answer. We head out and the sun is warm. It's the perfect day for a barbecue outside.

"Why, thank you," I tell him as he opens my door.

Leaning in, I kiss him, letting out the breath I've been holding for a long time. In every relationship I've ever been in, they've ended badly because I've either been lied to or cheated on. But with Nate, I think we've worked past all of the crap, and because of that, we're not gonna repeat what I've been through.

Deep down in the pit of my soul, my heart continues to pull me towards him and it's telling me that he is my future. He's done nothing but reassure me that he will never do anything to jeopardize that again.

We drive the short distance to pick up Nate's mom hand in hand, neither of us saying much, and for me today, that's okay. As Nate pulls his car in front of the facility, both of us are shocked to see his mom outside, and she's *not* sitting in her wheelchair either. She has a walker in front of her and is just beaming as she chats with one of the nurses.

"Holy fuck, El," he whispers putting the car in park. We look at each other, then get out of the car. Barb looks between Nate and I, then to the nurse who helps her stand up. Nate freezes and I stop next to him. We are both stunned as she begins to slowly walk towards us. Her steps are small, but her strength is apparent.

She stops right in front of Nate and reaches her arms for him. He hugs her tightly and I can see the tears flood from her eyes as she is in his arms. I myself cannot control the tears as I watch. Quickly, I wipe them away wanting to be strong for both of them.

Nate grabs my hand and pulls me over. "You are truly amazing, Barb," I tell her as we embrace.

"My son motivates me."

I catch Nate talking to the nurse. I'm sure it's

to work out the details of the transportation. He comes over to us and we all get loaded into his car and head off to his parents' house. As we begin to drive, I wonder how long it will take Barb to notice that we aren't going to the hospital.

As I wash the last of the dishes with Nate's cousin, I grin watching Nate, his dad, and mom all reunited in their home and so relaxed. Barb has the best laugh and is funny as hell. It's so great to see her up and in such good spirits. And to say that she was surprised when we brought her here is a complete understatement. She was speechless. Her smile was practically face-splitting as she broke down crying tears of joy.

"How long have you and Nate known each other?" Laura, his cousin, asks me.

"Just a couple months."

"I would have guessed you knew him long-er."

"Really? Why?"

"Just how comfortable you guys are together

and how much my aunt and uncle like you, especially with everything that he went through with, well, you know…"

She is referring to his ex, Arion, but I'm not even going to acknowledge anything regarding her. "Thanks for helping with the dishes," she says with a soft voice sensing she went too far with her big mouth when I don't answer her.

"Do you wanna head out back?"

"Oh…yeah."

We both walk out into the back yard, and as soon as I open the door, Nate's eyes are on mine, a huge smile is on his face when he sees me, and he pats his knee. I go to him and sit down, getting comfy in his arms.

"I missed you," he whispers in my ear.

Gently, I kiss his cheek. "I missed you more."

"Are you about ready to get going?"

I nod my head and get up as Nate directs me to stand. It seems to take us about fifteen minutes to say our goodbyes, but we finally do and head out. "Do you need to stop anywhere on the way home?"

"Nah, I don't think so."

"Good. Thank you for everything today, El. I

really don't think I could have made it through the day without you."

"Well, I had a wonderful time," I tell him, grabbing his hand. "Thank you for having me.

"Listen, I don't really know how to say this, but…" he trails off and it makes me nervous.

"Just say it." There's an underlying tone of frustration in my voice. It's probably because of the shit we have been through lately. I guess I'm still waiting for a bomb to drop.

"I want us to live together."

Did I just hear him right? "But you're closing on your place next week."

"I know, I'm just not as excited as I was about it before, if you're not going to be living there. Suddenly I don't want to start that chapter of my life without you."

His words stun me. I'm not sure how to respond. Living with Nate and having a home that is ours would truly be a dream come true. But I also know the harsh reality of making moves too quickly and what it can do to a relationship.

"What do you think?"

"I mean…I'd love that, but…"

"But what?" he asks, getting onto the freeway, clearly a little confused.

"I'm scared it's too soon. I'm scared that it will change things for us and ultimately, be the...the end."

"Nothing could change how I feel for you, El." He pulls the car over and as the wheels take their final spin coming to a complete stop, he unbuckles his seat belt and turns towards me, grabbing my hands.

"You don't know that, Nate."

"But I do. No matter what, nothing in this world could change the way I feel about you."

"Nate, I've done this, and moving in too soon can change things."

"Not for me it can't," he says.

"It can and right now, I don't want anything to change. We've been through so much already."

He pauses and I brace myself, afraid of what he is going to say. I watch him, obviously hurt, staring out the window.

"Okay," he says. "Nothing will change."

CHAPTER 26

-Nate-

As I sign document after document, my mind is a little preoccupied. I wish that today had a different outcome. But maybe Elania is right — maybe it is too soon for us to move in together.

At least right now, we do spend a lot of time together, basically just choosing whose place we will stay the night at. My phone rings and it's a number I don't recognize. I ignore the call, finishing up the last few items that I need to sign.

"Who's that?" Elania asks me.

"I don't know."

Then her phone rings and I see her face change. Glancing down, I notice it looks like the same number that just called me. "I'm gonna take this."

"Sure."

I watch her walk out, wondering who would have called both of us. As the closing comes to an end, she comes back in, with her usual confidence shining through.

"Congratulations, Mr. Wilcox," the closing agent says. We all shake hands and disburse from the room.

"Who was on the phone?"

"Just a client."

I cock one eyebrow at her, not buying what she's selling, but I let it go.

"Are you ready to go to your house?"

"I am."

We walk out holding hands and I notice that Elania seems to be more enthusiastic than I am. You would think that she's the one that just bought the condo, not me.

As I get into her Escalade, she asks me, "Are you excited?"

"Yeah. I guess."

"You guess?"

"I mean, I don't know."

"What's the matter?" she asks.

"Nothing," I reassure her. Well aware that bringing up the fact that I'd rather us be moving in today is nagging at the back of my mind, I also know it isn't going to help anything.

"Good. Then smile, dammit – this is your

first place."

"I am." I look at her and remember how damn lucky I am just to have her. *One day, we'll move in together.*

"We still need to go furniture shopping," she says.

"Yeah we do, I'm sorry I've been so busy lately. Maybe this weekend?"

"Works for me."

It's not but a few minutes 'til we are pulling up in front of my new home. It seems like forever since I have been here. *Damn, it's nice.* As Elania puts the vehicle in park, she turns in her seat and says, "I'm sorry that we aren't moving in today. I want you to know—"

I cut her off. "It's okay, babe." I can see the stress on her face. As much as I want her to explain, I also don't want her to hurt about the situation. Clearly my stress is wearing off on her. We talked about it the other night and deep down I realize that she's only hesitant because of her past. I want to do everything possible to make her comfortable with every step we take. Even if it's not exactly what I want, she's worth waiting for. I'll give her the time.

Leaning over she kisses me and then gets out

of the car. I follow suit and we walk up, Elania opens the door before I can get my key out of my pocket and I'm surprised that the condo is unlocked. She walks in, stepping in front of me and then turns to me with the biggest smile on her face. Glancing around, I can tell why. The condo is fully furnished. From the living room, to dining room, everything is brand new. There are still tags hanging from the furniture.

She waits for my response, but I'm fucking stunned. "You did this?" I ask.

"Of course."

"Why?"

"Why not?"

"Uhhh, because it had to have cost a ton of money."

"Nate, I used the money the sellers paid me. I wasn't about to keep that as a profit. I'm sorry that we aren't moving in today, I wish that it was different. But I can't make the same mistakes as I have in the past. Plus, you mean so much to me. It's not worth risking what we have."

I can't even respond to her. Her words are all I needed to hear. Grabbing her by the waist, I take her pants off and lift her on one of the new bar stools that she bought for me. She reaches for my pants, freeing my cock. I am hard and ready for her. Hell, I always am lately; she does this to me. She pulls me towards her, gripping the skin of my shaft, and I glide myself inside. Her warm cunt surrounds me as our eyes stay connected.

Once I am nestled to the hilt, I grab the back of her head and begin to move. Her noises fill the room and I know that no matter what, she is my future. Moving in today or not, we will be together.

"Fuck me, Nate."

Listening to her command, I grab the bar behind her. "Hold on to my neck," I tell her.

She gets a good grip and I fuck her, like she asked. Hard and strong thrusts. Christ, she brings out the animal in me. Her noises heighten with my movements. My balls slap her ass and I can't seem to push myself inside of her deep enough.

Her hands move to my back and are all over as she tightens her sweet cunt. Fuck, I'm close to coming. I can't last long with her. Automatically my eyes shut as I lose myself inside of her. My body lets go on its own and she follows suit coming hard on my cock, her muscles tightening around my shaft.

The room is filled with our noises and this is the first spot of many that we will have sex in. I lose all control and the reality of the world slips away. Looking down at her as I slowly stroke myself inside of her, she is leaning back, still clinging to me. I look further down and watch my cock move in and out of her.

Her pussy is wrapped so tightly around me that I etch this moment in my memory before pulling all the way out. Elaina giggles as she runs off to the restroom, leaving her pants on the floor. "You should run naked more often," I say as I readjust myself.

"If I had a treadmill, I would."

I take her pants into the bathroom. "I have a better idea."

"Yeah?"

"Let's do a work out at the gym after hours."

She laughs at me as if I'm joking, then breaks off. "Oh, fuck, you're serious."

I nod my head. "Nash is going out of town 'til next week. He, Amanda, and I are the only ones with keys to the gym. So I'll tell her what we're doing and she'll be sure to stay away."

"I don't know, Nate."

"Why not? No one is gonna see us. That

place is a brick fortress." I button her pants as she stands up and lean into her neck. "Please."

"You really want this, huh?"

I nod my head.

"Fine, but no one better catch us."

I take my index finger and cross it over my heart. She kisses it and takes my hand, leading me through the rest of the house. She really outdid herself. I have a hard time believing that she was able to buy everything with just the money that she made off of the sale of the house. But she's adamant that she did, so I believe her.

"Thank you for doing all of this."

"Absolutely. Thank you for understanding where I'm coming from."

Leaning down, I kiss her and want to fuck her again. She stops me, pressing her forefinger against my lips and I about bite it off. "I have to get back to work. I'm sorry, but I have an appointment this afternoon." I growl in protest, but nod my head in agreement. "Let's stay here tonight and celebrate," she says.

"Okay," I respond and walk outside. I lock up and my phone vibrates as I slide the key into my pocket. Before I get into the car, I check it, and my stomach drops...it's Andrea.

CHAPTER 27

-Elania-

What does one wear to work out naked? I chuckle thinking about what we are about to do. I really can't believe that I am going to go through with this.

Walking up to my house, Nate is sitting outside on his phone. I really have to give him a key; After all, I have a key to his place. He gets out of his car and walks towards me. That shit-eating grin is all over his face. "You too, Ma. I will." He kisses me and then squeezes my ass.

I swat his hand. "Okay, bye." He hangs up and says, "My mom said to tell you she appreciates the book recommendation."

"Oh, I'm glad. How was your day?" I ask him as we walk inside.

"It was okay. I missed you and dealt with a hard dick all day in anticipation of tonight."

I laugh out loud. "Did you now?"

He nods his head eyeing me up and down. I love it when he looks at me this way. "What?" I ask, always wanting to know what he's thinking.

"Nothing, just enjoying the view."

"Right," I retort. "Do you want to eat here before we go?"

"Fuck, dinner. I'll be eating you. I'm ready to go now."

"I need to change."

"Why? You'll be naked."

I roll my eyes at him while grabbing us two smoothies from the fridge. "Fine, let's go."

"After you," he says, standing with his apparent hard on showing itself to me.

On the drive, I notice that both of us are extremely quiet. For me, I'm nervous. I've never dreamt of doing anything like this and I'm scared someone is gonna catch us. For Nate, God only knows what he's thinking.

"What is *this* workout gonna entail?" I ask.

"A little of everything, and if you do whatever I ask, maybe I'll reward you."

"I like rewards."

"Do you now?"

My mind drifts, thinking about all of the possibilities for tonight. Before long, Nate puts the car into park and is out and opening my door. Getting out, his dick is still hard. I smirk at his pants. Apparently, he doesn't like that and readjusts himself before dragging me upstairs.

Unlocking the door to the gym, the cleaners are just finishing. "Hey, Jose."

"Mr. Wilcox," the man responds in his thick accent. "We were just finishing up."

"Thanks. Did you get everything done that I asked for?"

"We did." Nate shakes his hand and I stand back looking around nervously. He had the place fucking cleaned for this? This is serious.

"No need to set the alarm; I will when we leave."

The cleaners all scurry about and then disperse from the building, as Nate heads into the office and gestures me in after him. He fiddles around on the computer, then says, "Cameras are off. Now...I'm gonna lock up and I want you naked when I get back.

I swallow watching him tear his shirt above his head before he leaves me. I look around anxiously, then remember that the gym is on the second level, so unless someone scales up the side of the building, no one is going to see us. I don't take much time getting undressed. Just as I figure out where to stand or sit, I catch Nate staring at me. He is naked and oh so fucking hot. I clamp my legs together from the simple sight of him. He's so sexy as he walks towards me.

"On the desk." I look next to me, but before I can move, he lifts me onto the cool metal surface of the retro desk. I gasp from the cold chill on my thighs. "I've wanted to fuck you on this desk for so long. Did you know that?"

I shake my head. His eyes, so dark and serious as he sinks inside of me. "Oh, fuck," I cry out.

"Yes, let me hear you."

And then our night begins and he shows no mercy pounding me. My body moves with his and I give him this moment, this is about him and not me. He's been horny all day for this and I know in order to please him I need to take a good fucking; he needs his release. Giving all that I am over to him, I don't even think about myself, only Nate.

"Yes, fuck me hard."

He growls looking down at me and presses one hand over my stomach. I wrap my legs tightly around his body, glowing in his presence, willing and waiting for him to let go. "Harder," I ask.

His eyes widen as he slows a bit. "I love it when you tell me what you want, El." He's breathless and hot as hell.

"Good, now fuck me 'til you come inside of me."

His stare remains intense, followed by his long thrusts. Then, his pace begins to quicken and he tilts his head back letting go and grunting with each thrust. I find pleasure in watching him come so well, knowing that this is just the beginning of what the night has in store for me.

Nate leans down and sucks each of my nipples, pulling on them. I arch into him and groan in protest when he pulls out of me. I love it when he's inside of me.

He hands me a few tissues and waits for me to clean myself up. Then we walk out into the gym. He flips on all of the lights and asks, "Are you ready?"

"As I'll ever be."

He kisses my hand and we go over to the long row of treadmills. "Shoes on for this," he reminds me. I jog to the office where I retrieve then. I can sense that his eyes are watching me. Never faltering, I make sure that I bend over to put them on with my naked ass in full view.

Strutting back towards Nate, he starts up a treadmill for me, which I hop right on and begin a brisk walk, he moves all around the machine, watching me from every angle while moving the speed up. I keep my eyes on him and his amazing cock and the way that he stares at me. He's completely immersed in me.

He slows the machine down and I hop off. "Fuck, you're hot. How did I get so lucky?"

"I could say the same thing." He begins to walk off and I clear my throat. He turns towards me and I gesture that it's his turn on the tread-mill.

"For real?" he asks.

"Yup, how fast can you go?"

"As fast as you want."

I keep the speed slow, wanting to get a good view of how his body moves. Each step moves his cock so easily. He doesn't last long before he hits the stop button. I can tell tonight won't be fair, but that's okay, I'll take what I can get of him. As the night progresses, we bounce all around the gym, from machine to machine, both of us laughing and having a good time just being free, while the space between us is filled with nothing but sexual tension.

"Sit on the ball," I order.

He looks at the round yellow yoga ball and basically laughs at me. "No way."

"Why?" I challenge with my hands on my hips.

"Uh, 'cause it's dirty."

"Well, that's your fault if you didn't have everything cleaned. Go grab some Clorox wipes, because I've always wanted to fuck on one of these." He slaps my ass, jogging to the office, clearly agreeing with my decision.

After he thoroughly cleans the ball, he rests it against one of the weight benches before sitting down. With nothing but desire in his eyes, he looks me up and down. "On your knees on the weight bench first."

I obey, like I have been doing all night and get on my knees, placing my hands on my thighs. Nate walks to the end of the bench with his fist clenched around his cock. I scoot a little forward and wrap my lips around his head, engulfing every part of him. As I suck him, I look up to see him watching me carefully. Staring particularly close at my lips. "I love it when your mouth's around my cock," he says.

"Yeah?" I ask, pulling away.

"Uh-huh," he confirms and I direct him to sit on the ball, straddling my body over him, looking down at the closeness between us. His cock is throbbing and ready to fuck me while my pussy can't wait. Taking my time, I move slowly nuzzling down on him 'til he fills me completely.

"This is my favorite kind of workout," I tell him.

He looks down at my tight cunt wrapped all around him and pumps himself inside of me, using the bounce of the ball under his ass to his advantage. "Me too."

I moan in pleasure, locking my fingers behind his head as we move together. Caressing his shaft with my softness and warmth. Heat emits through my entire body, burning from my head to my toes. Nate meets me thrust for thrust, filling me as deep as I can take. With each movement, I let my body fall deeper. Ecstasy consumes me and we both savor this time, each other, and what our bodies do together.

"I'm going to miss you so bad," I tell Nate as I cuddle against him.

"Me too, baby. How long will you be gone for?" he asks me.

"Three days."

He kisses my neck and we lie in silence for a while. Neither of us says a thing. Inside, I know that I am completely falling for him. As much as I try to be cautious and fight it...I can't. I am completely smitten. I've tried to not let myself end up in this situation, but here I am.

"Can I take you to breakfast before you leave?" he asks.

I nod my head wondering if I should tell him about my feelings now. But before I can ponder on the subject anymore, Nate slides on top of me, kissing my neck – his sweet lips so soothing. Closing my eyes, I wind my fingers into his hair holding on as he moves his way down my body.

Finally after touching every bit of my skin, he settles between my legs. My body bows beneath him, waiting for him to touch me. But he doesn't. Instead he breathes on me, blowing a smooth trail of warm air on my hot skin.

Needing more, I push my sex against him willing him to give in to me. It works like a charm and he does. The second that he touches me, my body is filled with nothing but pure bliss. He groans, flicking his tongue back and forth, and in this moment, I get lost in him.

Reaching my hand down, I search for his cock to hold and stroke. My knees are slacked as he's comfortably between them. But he can tell what I'm searching for and he stops licking, placing his hard shaft right in the palm of my hand. Looking down at me, there's a look in his eye that I've not seen before. I watch as his muscles flex from me persistently pleasuring him. He stays kneeling and I don't let up. He's watching what I am doing and only lasts a second before he hovers over me again, scooting to me on his knees. As soon as his dick is in reach of my mouth, I take it in, feeling every ridge that makes him impeccable.

Resting his hands on his sides, his head is tilted back and I work my magic. His noises are so hot, such a low grunt from deep within his throat. He turns me on and I tighten my pussy looking for any friction and to my surprise, Nate reaches back and rewards me with exactly what I have been looking for.

I gasp out loud and stop sucking him. He watches how the pleasure rolls through me. My body arches and I continue to stroke his shaft, whimpering from his touch.

"Can I fuck you?" he asks me.

"Please," I practically beg, accepting him as he moves down and pushes his way deep inside of me. Warmth shoots through me, from my head to my toes. Nate cups my face, settling his body above mine. In this moment with him, he is all that I have ever wanted; he satisfies me in a way no other man ever has. It's just one of the reasons that solidifies that I am falling for him and…I can't wait to tell him.

CHAPTER 28

-Nate-

My phone keeps ringing and for some God unknown reason, it's Andrea. I'm pissed beyond words that she's putting me in this situation. Not only is she calling me, but Amanda said she went into the gym asking for me. I told her not to contact me and I was honest in the fact that we had no future. That I'd moved on with El. But here I am dealing with her crazy ass persistence, all while trying to enjoy breakfast with Elania before she leaves town.

"The coffee here is so good," she says holding the huge cup in her small hands.

"Yeah, it is." I don't mean to be short, but Andrea has my head twisted. Inside, I know I should tell Elania, but…I can't. I can't bring up the whole situation again, especially when we have come so far and she's about to leave town. I don't want her to have doubts when we are apart.

"Are you two ready to order?" the waitress asks us.

I look to El, and she spouts off what we want. Man, I'm grateful how well she knows me already. I stare at her, she's so gorgeous. And today she seems different, really comfortable with us. Finally she's putting her walls down again, but I'm disconnected. *Damn Andrea.* Hopefully Elania won't catch on.

"Are you okay today?" she asks me.

Shit. "Yeah, why?" I immediately respond.

"You're quiet."

I grab her hands over the table to let her know that I'm good. She looks deep into my eyes. "I…I think I might be getting sick," I lie. Knowing right away that it's wrong, but it'll explain my quietness.

"Really? I'm sorry."

"It's all right. I might not be, I just feel a little off."

"I can cancel my trip. Mads, would totally understand."

"Absolutely not," I demand. "She's your cousin and this is her time. Go and enjoy her bachelorette party."

"You sure you don't want me to stay?" she

asks.

"Yeah."

"Okay. What do you think if when I get back we…" She trails off, looking down at our intertwined hands.

"What?" I ask nervously swallowing hard. All of a sudden, she doesn't look herself.

"Can we talk about taking the next step and moving in together?"

I can't believe what she's saying. Am I hearing her right? I sit there dumbfounded for a few minutes, which feels like an eternity. I need to say something, but I'm speechless. Honestly…lost for words.

"What…" I stop, swallowing hard. "What made you change your mind?"

"I don't know how to explain it, Nate." She lifts my hand, kissing my knuckles. "I guess it's just a feeling."

"El, I'd love nothing more than to move in together, you know that. So if you wanna talk about it when you get back, that's fine with me."

She smiles from ear to ear. The waitress interrupts us, setting our food down, and I'm bereft at having to let go of her hands. But I find solitude in the look in her eyes – it's still there. I can't believe she's ready. If it were up to me, I'd move her in right now. But I've learned my lesson with pushing the subject. This time, I'm leaving the ball in her court. She has her reservations, whatever they are, and that's okay. I won't push her. If she says that she wants to talk about it when she's back, then that's what we'll do.

After breakfast with El, I watched her pack and now just dropped her off at the airport. During it all, my phone never ceased ringing. It got to the point that I had to turn it off. As I drive away from the airport, I turn it back on and am contemplating calling Andrea. But then I decide against it. I can picture El's face if she knew and I cannot bear to disappoint her.

I decide to call Amanda instead. It takes her a few moments to answer, but finally she does.

"I need some advice."

"What's the matter? Things okay with Elania?"

"Yeah, things are really good. She actually said she wants to move in together."

"Really? That's great news. What's the matter then?"

"Andrea started blowing my phone up again."

"Fuck. What's her deal?"

"I have no idea. I wasn't nice to her the last time I saw her, and she knows about El, so I don't know what she wants."

"Nate, you need to tell her that what she's doing isn't okay. Especially since you and Elania are doing so well. Did you tell Elania?"

"Fuck, no. Hang on." My other line is ringing, I check to see that it's Andrea's number. "It's her again."

"You gotta be firm with her and handle it. Stop avoiding it in hopes that she'll go away. Because clearly, she won't."

"Thanks, Amanda, I'll call her."

"Oh, Nate, you might want to tell Elania about it all, too."

We hang up and I know she's right, but I just don't want to do that with her being so far away. Heading down the freeway, a text chimes in on my phone; it's El. *Just boarded my plane, turning my phone off…for now. I'll call you when I land.*

As I get off on my exit, I contemplate calling

Andrea. But I figure I better have a little game plan before getting knee deep in the shit-storm that is her life.

What I want to do right now is tell her that I am absolutely not fucking interested in her or anything that has to do with her. I've basically said that, but maybe if I am a little harsher this time, she'll get my damn point.

Then…she calls, again. I answer, knowing that I just have to get this over with. There is no game plan that can help me; I just need to be a royal asshole.

"Why the fuck are you calling me?" I ask, my annoyance blatantly obvious.

"Thank God you answered Nate. Please don't hang up on me."

"Why the hell not? I told you, Andrea, I've moved on and I am not interested. You're going to cause a problem for me."

"I know, I know, trust me, that's not why I'm calling. It's Ronnie, he's lost his fucking mind. He beat the shit out of me and—"

I cut her off. "What? Why? Are you okay?"

"Yeah, I'm all right."

"What's his deal?"

"I think he started taking drugs again after I broke up with him. He's acting like a lunatic."

"Fuck," I blurt out, not knowing how to respond to her.

"I've been trying to get ahold of you, because he said he was gonna find you and beat the shit out of you too."

I can't help but laugh. "I doubt that, but let him try. I have some built up anger needing a release."

"Nate, I'm serious. Be careful. He knows that you own Mechanical."

"I will, don't worry. Have you reported this to the police?"

"No, that's the last thing that I need."

"Why the fuck not?" I ask, so baffled that I want to hang up on her dumb ass.

"I have a warrant out for my arrest, because I didn't go to court for an old speeding ticket." *What the fuck? This chick is crazy.*

"Uh, okay. Well, be safe and take care of yourself. I'll be around this weekend if anything happens, but then that's it. I mean it, Andrea."

She sounds completely genuine in her tone and a small part of me actually feels bad for her.

Pulling up to Mechanical, I take an extra look over my shoulder to make sure this fucker isn't around looking for an ass whooping, but it seems I'm in the clear…for now.

CHAPTER 29

-Elania-

Being in Florida is so different from Jersey. The city we're in is so small and it's right on the beach. The weather is HOT, and the humidity is something else. But I could stay forever, even with the differences…if Nate were here. Walking back into the hotel, I'm linked arm and arm with Mads and I can tell she's ecstatic that I'm here.

It's all because of Nate. He pushed me to come and I couldn't be happier. I'm not one for bachelorette parties, but he's right – you do only get married once. "Any more pictures of your hot ass boyfriend come in?" Kassy asks me as I check my phone.

"No, I wish. He's not feeling well today."

"That's okay. Mads says he can send us one from bed."

"Mads," I scold her, "You're about to get

married."

"What? He's fucking gorgeous and this is my last single weekend." I giggle at the girls. They are all smitten with him, the same way that I am. However, I do feel bad for him. He sounded horrible on the phone earlier and it really took me out of my element tonight. As much as I wanted to have a good time, he was all I could think about.

Getting back into the room, I sneak into the bathroom and call him. There's no answer and I assume it's because he's sleeping. As I begin to leave a message, he calls me back.

"Hey baby," he says in a quiet tone.

"Hey, how are you?" I ask.

"I'm okay. Sorry, I was sleeping."

"No worries, are feeling any better?" I ask, fiddling with a lotion bottle.

"No, I think this cold hit me hard."

"Have you taken anything for it?"

"Nah, there's no medicine that can help me right now."

Nate yawns loudly and I figure I better let him sleep. At the same time, I feel just as tired.

"Well, I can't wait to see you tomorrow.

"Me too. Goodnight, baby."

We hang up and as I leave the bathroom, everyone is passed out. Well everyone except for Monica. I chuckle looking at all the girls, spread out everywhere.

Did they really drink that much? I guess so, as silence fills the room.

Knowing I'll have you in my bed tonight makes today that much easier. I wake to Nate's text message and take this quiet opportunity to text him back. **I wish it was this morning. How are you feeling?"**

Pretty shitty, but I'm just gonna stay in bed all day and sleep.

I'll be there soon. Little does Nate know that "soon" means in a few hours. Last night, Monica's husband texted her because their son is sick. She decided to go home early today and I took the opportunity to skip out with her. All that I'll be missing is a day at the pool and pedicures. Mads' bachelorette celebrations are long over.

Slowly, the other girls start to wake. All of

them look ridiculous with their messy hair and smeared make-up. Not to mention that they are still dressed for a night out. Glancing at the clock, I'm worried with how much of a mess these girls are that we'll make it to breakfast in time.

I search for Mads and find her banging on the bathroom door, yelling at Kassy who's clearly puking her guts out.

"How are you feeling?" I ask her.

"I'm fine, I just have to piss and this twat drank too much and is now ruining my morning," she screams through the door.

"Mads, look around. I think everyone drank too much. Granted, there are a few of us that can handle it better than others."

"True. So did you decide to go home early?"

"Yeah, I was able to change my flight with Monica so we are gonna leave after breakfast."

"Okay. How's Nate?"

"Not too well. I think it will be good to get home and take care of him."

"I do too."

Kassy finally unlocks the bathroom door and comes stumbling out. She almost misses the bed, falling face first onto the plush white comforter.

I hug Mads before she flies in. Then pack up everything into my suitcase. My phone chimes with a text from Nate.

I miss you, El.

I miss you more, Nate. Get some rest.

After we all somehow manage to eat, Monica and I make our way to the airport. Monica is rambling on and on about her husband and son. Don't get me wrong, I love to hear how happy she is, but inside I wonder if I will ever have what she has, and if so…will it be with Nate?

I want nothing more, but in my past something has always screwed up what I've wanted. Especially when things seem to be going well. Now I'm scared to hope for things to go my way. I have to remind myself to not let my past dictate my future. And I hold faith that it won't happen with Nate, that we will have a future just like Monica does. A future I've always dreamed of.

CHAPTER 30

-Nate-

"How are you holding up?" Andrea asks me.

I shake my head, completely disgusted with myself. If Elania had any idea that Andrea was at my house right now, she would never talk to me again. But when Andrea called *again*, hysterical and afraid, I regretted saying I was available to her for the weekend, but I couldn't leave her to die either. She was sobbing so hard I could barely make out the words and her voice trembled with obvious terror after that asshole threatened to kill her. I couldn't turn her away. Especially because she is in this situation because of me. Me and my stupid dick.

"Has he stopped texting you?" I ask her.

"Yeah, for now."

"What are you thinking you're gonna do?"

"I called my aunt in Oregon, and she said I can come stay with her, so I was gonna take a bus."

"That's crazy; I'll pay for a flight."

She rests her chin atop her knee and stares out my back window. "No, Nate, you've done enough. I already feel terrible being here."

My phone chimes with a text from El, *I hope you're sleeping well, I'm going to the pool with the girls. I'll call you later.*

Have fun, baby, I miss you, I text her back with a heavy heart.

"I'm sorry to put you in this situation and that we can't go to the cops."

"It's all right. Getting you out of here safely is what matters to me at this point."

"Thanks. Hey, Nate?"

"Yeah?" I ask staring at Elania's text.

"I'm happy for you."

Looking over at Andrea, I realize I'm smiling at my phone. "Thanks."

Grabbing my iPad, I pass it to her, "Here, find yourself a flight and I'll pay for it."

She doesn't argue. She knows that she needs to leave town quickly for her safety. She also knows that I have to get El from the airport tonight and she's got to be gone. I'm not trying to justify Andrea being here, but she doesn't want to make things worse and I appreciate that right now.

"Do you want more coffee?" I ask her.

She nods her head, her hair sheeting around her face just like Arion's and I remember why I liked her, what seems to be so long ago. I cannot believe how time changes our perspective on things. Thinking back on where I was just a few short months ago, it honestly doesn't seem like my life. From reeling in the pain of losing Arion and thinking that I could never move on to dulling the pain with Andrea, and using her in every wrong way possible. Then out of the blue, Elania, my El.

I pass Andrea her coffee and ask, "Did you find anything?"

"There's a flight that leaves at one o'clock today."

"That's great, book it."

"You didn't even ask how much it is."

"Doesn't matter, not one bit, as long as you're safe and as far away from that asshole as possible."

"Thank you, Nate. That's all that I want too." Her expression is genuine, and with that, I get up to grab my wallet. I notice her phone vibrating on the counter. It's Ronnie, and my rage rises so fast that I answer it without thinking.

"What the fuck do you want?"

He laughs in his high-pitched tone. "So she's with you?"

"Is that a problem? From what I heard, you beat the shit out of her and left her bleeding on the bathroom floor."

"Is that what she said? Did she tell you why?"

I laugh out loud. "There's no excuse, bitch. Only a coward would hit a woman."

"Call me what you want, you one-legged freak. You'd do the same thing if she pulled the shit with you that she did with me."

"Watch your mouth, asshole."

"Or what?" he challenges.

"I guess you'll have to find out," I snarl.

"Just tell Andrea that I'm not finished with her."

"Nah, I'm not gonna do that because you *are* finished with her. If you know what's good for you." My tone is as serious as ever and Andrea stands in front of me, wide-eyed panic spread across her face. "Do you hear me? If you so much as try and contact her one more time, I'll track you down and twist your fucking neck."

He begins to laugh hysterically and I take it upon myself to just hang up. There's no reason to keep fucking with this douchebag. I'm so pissed, but relieved I made my point. Although when I look at Andrea she's shaking her head back and forth like I've done something wrong, when all along all I've wanted to do was try and protect her.

I grab my credit card and pass it to her, not really caring what she has to say. I can tell that she's pissed, but someone needed to set that douchebag straight.

She takes the card and whispers, "Thank you."

After Andrea reserves her flight and gets her shit together, we get on the road. "Thank you for everything, Nate, I hope you know how much it means to me that you let me come here."

"I'm just glad that you're okay. I'm sorry if I was an asshole at all."

"I understand."

"Thanks, Andrea."

I glance at her out of the corner of my eye, her long, blonde hair is shower wet and messy. I really wish her nothing but the best...she probably doesn't even realize the depth of the shit that she put up with from me during the whole time we were fucking around. She deserves to get away not only from the douchebag, but also me. The rest of the drive we sit in silence, both of us lost in our own minds. Mine is focused on Elania. Finally, tonight, I get to see her. It seems so long ago that she left, even though it's only been a few short days.

I really can't wait to have her in my arms. Her light eyes and dark hair consume me. I can hear her voice and envision her lips against mine. Pulling up to the airport, relief washes over me. This is the end, and I can't wait to put this all behind me. Soon Andrea will be safe, and I'm hoping after the talk I had with Ronnie that he will really leave her alone. She truly does deserve it.

Parking in front of the departure area for her airline, I wish Andrea, "Good luck." And she leans over hugging me. I hug her back, knowing she's been through a lot.

"I'm sorry for the way that things have turned out."

"Please don't be," she says over my shoulder. "You have no idea how much I appreciate everything." We pull away and I can see fear written all over her face.

"Be strong. You're going to be thousands of miles away; he can't hurt you." She nods her head and we get out of the car. Freedom is only seconds away.

CHAPTER 31

-Elania-

"Jesus, that flight was brutal," Monica says resting her head against the seat, looking shaken and a little green.

"I never used to mind flying, but after that I might rethink how I travel."

Both Monica and I turn our phones on. There is a lot of chatter amongst the cabin, everyone complaining about the turbulence. We're not the only ones who are upset about the flight. Monica gets on the phone with her husband and I contemplate texting Nate, but I decide against it. He's sleeping, and besides, I really want to surprise him. He thinks I'm at the pool with the girls and that's how it'll stay.

I gather my things trying not to listen to Monica on the phone, but she's so damn cute. She and her husband have been together forever.

They are one of the first couples that I met when I moved here from California and come to find out that Monica and Mads went to college together.

"How's Koby?" I ask her.

"Poor little guy…he's about the same. Jason said his fever hasn't broken and he's still really lethargic."

As everyone starts to exit the plane we grab our belongings and head out as well. "I'm sorry he's sick, girl."

"He's gonna be okay, I just turn into a total hypochondriac the second my baby has the tiniest sniffle, but I can't control it."

"If you wanna get going home, you can. I totally understand and can catch a cab."

"Are you sure?" she asks.

"Of course, get home and take care of your little boy."

The elevator dings and we get out, looking around. I see a sign for the parking garage and point to it. She hugs me before heading off.

"Let me know how Koby is."

"I will," she responds.

We separate and I walk out the nearest doors, needing to get a breath of fresh air. The hot New

Jersey summer day warms my skin, but the sight in front of me instantly knocks the air from my lungs. I stop dead in my tracks and have to do a double take.

I'm horrified as I watch Nate hugging another woman in his car. My chest staggers in pain. Every ounce of breath is stripped from my airway. This cannot be happening.

I shake my head not believing my eyes, tears form watching him get out of his car and walk to the trunk where he removes...her bags.

I second guess everything for a minute. There is no way it's Nate. But I know deep down, it is. It's his car, his license plate, his walk...everything. Dammit, it's *him*. My eyes move back to the girl, trying to figure out who it is. Then it hits me as my mind clicks back to the night when Andrea called him and her picture came up on his phone. I choke back a scream when I realize he's with her. He hugs her again and my worst fucking nightmare plays out in front of me. She leans in to kiss him.

Oh my fucking God. I consider confronting him but decide against it. Before I collapse and let another man do to me what Alex did, I bail. The walls spring back up around my heart and put it on lockdown. Nate doesn't deserve me or the time of day after such betrayal. Looking back at them, he catches sight of me and freezes. His face turns white, like he's looking at a ghost. My face is covered in disgust and I hope he can see it.

I scramble into a cab waiting at the arrivals area and hear Nate yelling for me as he runs for the cab. "To Scotch Plains," I command the driver.

The cabbie pulls away, starting the meter. Not a word is spoken from him. Which for me right now is best. I'm lost in my head. I can't look at Nate again. Thinking about everything sets me to heaving in a fit of tears. My biggest fear has just come true. Never in a million years did I imagine Nate would lie to me…again. Or turn to another woman over me the way that Alex did, but he's done it.

My breathing is so short and I don't know how to make anything better. My world is crumbling around me. *Deep breaths, just calm down,* I repeat in my head hoping that sheer force of will can keep me from collapsing 'til I am home.

I do my best to listen to myself, closing my eyes to regain some control, but all I see is Nate and that girl. What he was doing with her was normal, comfortable, like they do it all the time. I mean, he dropped her off the same way he dropped me off, just three days prior. *He's been cheating on me all along,* is all that floods my mind.

I take a few deep breaths to keep trying to calm myself down, then my phone vibrates. I know it's Nate. I can't even bring myself to check it. He's just going to give me some BS excuse and lie the way he apparently always does.

My phone vibrates again and I can tell he's not going to make this easy, but there is no excuse for what he's done. Plain and simple. I just have to stay strong and not give in to him. He texts again and I glance at the screen reading the string of messages.

El, please call me.

It's not what you think.

I was just trying to help her, nothing happened.

I ignore him, now knowing that he's a fucking liar. *Baby, please!* he texts as I stare at my phone. Fuck him. Goddamn Nate Wilcox. "Nothing happened" – is he serious? I saw it with my own eyes. I watched him drop some slut he used to bang off after kissing her good-bye and doing lord only knows what else with her. We're fuckin' done.

CHAPTER 32

-Nate-

I'd expected that once I dropped Andrea off at the airport, a wave of relief would wash over me. Finally, she'd be gone and out of my life. With nothing ahead of me but my future with Elania. But everything went so, so wrong today. Now, here I am in the most fucked up spot there is, missing her more than I ever knew was possible.

This whole situation was going to be the last lie – ever. Going forward, I was going to be one hundred percent honest with her no matter what. I'd been scared of her reaction if I told her the truth, afraid she'd leave me…which makes me sound like a real pussy, but I can't explain it, I think of telling her, and I'd do anything to avoid the panic that starts to rise.

Right now, for Elania, I'd face it though. I'm sick to my stomach, but honestly my stomach pain is no match compared to the mindfuck I'm in right now believing that it was the right thing to do, to protect her. There was no point to drag her down that road again. Clearly, a load of shit.

Thinking about her face when we made eye contact kills me. I cannot believe I ruined things.

I still haven't heard back from Elania and it's making me nervous. I need her to tell me that we'll make it through this. We will – after some time – right? Needing some perspective on the situation, I decide to call Nash. I'm too ashamed to call my mom and I can't call Amanda – she told me to be honest will El. Plus, he's been through a lot with relationships, so I'm hoping he can help.

"Sexy?" he answers.

"No, ass wipe, it's your partner."

"Yeah, my sexy partner."

"Does Jessica know that you talk to me like that?" I ask, irritated.

"Of course she does, she's lying here right now."

"Hi, Nate," she yells in the background.

"Hey, Jess." She giggles and I'm sure that the two of them are fucking around in bed. "I won't keep ya, bro, but I need some advice. I fucked up."

"What did you do now?"

I exhale, pulling up to my house. I'd contemplated going to hers, but I'll give it a little time before I do that. "I lied to Elania."

"Again, you dumb fuck?" he shouts.

"Uh-huh."

"What about now?"

"Andrea, that chick I was seeing a while ago. Her ex flipped out and…he beat the fuck out of her. I tried to help her, but didn't tell El and she caught me." I get out of the car and head into my house.

"Nate, what's your deal with lying, man?" I go to answer him, but something else stops me dead in my tracks.

"Hands up, motherfucker, and drop the phone," a short, stocky shadow says from behind me.

I stop, thinking about all of my options. I pretend to hang up, and set my phone face down on the floor. Standing back up with my hands in the air, I look straight ahead. All I can hope is that Nash, even as dumb as he is, will catch on and send help.

My mind switches to wondering who this guy is and why he's here. I think about my safe and how much money I have in it. Dammit, I don't think there's shit for cash in it right now.

"Good. Now where is she?"

"Who?" I ask, skipping from money to his question. Then all at once – it clicks. This is Andrea's crazy ass boyfriend. At first I contemplate playing dumb, but he's in my home, with a gun, and he's not leaving 'til he has answers.

"She's gone, bro."

"I'm not buying it."

"Well, it's the truth."

"Tell me where the fuck she is," he yells walking around me to face me.

His face is all jacked up, he's clearly been using again. "I dropped her off at the airport."

He looks me up and down, "Really? Where is she headed?"

I size him up. I could totally take him, even if he shoots me. I don't think it would be any worse than the roadside bomb that almost blew me to shreds.

"Why don't you put the gun down and fight me like a man, then I'll tell you."

"Nah, I'd rather watch you suffer." And he shoots at me. My ears ring from the blast of the gun shot. But I'm not hit. He's apparently a lousy shot, lucky for me. So I act quickly, taking a chance and lunge at him. Heat radiates down my arm, shocking me.

My ears ring again, and this time, he really got me. Falling to my knees, my hand flies to my shoulder and I heave for air, the shot pulling the air from my lungs.

"Look at me," he orders.

On hearing those words, I'm with my fucking captors again. "Look at me," he screams. I pull my eyes from the floor to meet his, struggling not to shut down completely, but there's a buzzing growing in my head threatening to black me out. His red eyes are glazed over; he's completely spun out of his mind.

He steps closer to me, never breaking eye contact.

"Now tell me, where the fuck is she?"

"Fuck you!" I yell at him and look away. My life flashes before my eyes and I wonder after all that I have been through, if this is how I will die. After surviving for almost a year half-dead and alone in Afghanistan to conquering it all and coming back. Is this how it will all end?

Fighting to stay upright, I keep pressure on my arm. Thinking about how I can still take him down. Then he presses the cold metal of the barrel against my forehead and I shut my eyes. *Fuck, I'm helpless.* The pain and fear are debilitating. But I pull Elania into my mind's eye, letting her fill every ounce of me. If this is my time to go, then I want to go with my thoughts consumed with her, not looking into the eyes of some sick freak.

The report of the gun again blasts through the room and I prepare to take my last breath.

You know that sensation when something hurts so bad that it's not pain at all? This is that feeling. Instead of pain, my body is covered with a heavy weight and my breathing slowly fades. I guess before you really die this is what happens. But before I let go, I hold on to Elania's sweet face. Her plump lips, light eyes, and…

"Dammit, Nate, wake up!" I recognize the voice, but don't understand how I'm hearing it. I will my eyes to open and see Nash above me. He is covered in blood and looks completely distraught.

"Nash?" I ask, so confused.

"It's me, man. You're gonna be okay. Jess, grab some more towels," he screams at her with tears in his eyes.

Then an enormous pressure takes over and I yell out in pain.

"I know, man, I'm sorry. Just hang in there."

I reach for my face, wondering how I've survived. Everything feels normal. It's...so strange, then another wave of pain takes over, but this time I can't hold on, losing my grasp...I fade away...

CHAPTER 33

-*Elania*-

"Just come home, El," my mom pleads into the phone.

"I want to, trust me, but I can't just pick up and leave."

"You can. There's nothing there for you in that godforsaken town except for Mads. Every man you've been with has broken your heart. I'm tired of all of these phone calls with you always upset."

"Mom, I appreciate you being so concerned about me, I really do, but I think I just wanna sleep on it and then I'll decide what I'm going to do tomorrow.

She sighs, but relents. "Okay, dear, but please call me if you need anything."

"I will. I promise."

My other line rings and I answer the unknown number without even thinking.

"Elania, it's Nash."

Annoyed that Nate put him up to this, I say, "Nash, please don't get in the middle of this."

"I'm not trying to get in the middle of any-thing."

"Well, you called."

"I had to. Elania, I don't know how else to say this, but…Nate's in the hospital."

The pain I felt earlier is nothing compared to this. *The hospital?* Right away, I get up, grab my keys, and dart for the door. "What happened?" I demand, getting into my car.

"He was shot. We're at New Jersey Medical Center. You have to get down here. It's serious."

I hang up, peeling out of my driveway. Adrenaline moves me. Nate was shot? How? Why? Christ, my mind races. Vomit creeps up in my throat and the events of the day all wash away as his life hangs in the balance. All at once, I don't care what he's done. I can't lose him. I fucking love him, dammit. Thankfully, the roads are clear and I take the opportunity to drive as fast as possible, whipping and winding as I make my way.

Nash's words replay in my head, haunting

me. *Please God, don't take him away from me.* It's not long 'til I arrive at the hospital and park in a panic, rushing into the ER. The man behind the desk glares at me, and with insistent eyes, I tell him, "I'm here to see Nate Wilcox."

He types on the keyboard, hitting the keys harder than is necessary, every key stroke feeling like an eternity, but before he can answer me, Nash emerges from behind the closed doors. My hand flies over my mouth as I watch him and Jess walk out. He has his arm over her shoulder and both of them are covered in blood.

"Nash," I yell, running to them, worry consuming me. "How is he?" I ask.

They both hug me. "He's alive and stable, thankfully."

"How did this happen?" Right now, I'm not even sure that matters, but the more I know, the better.

"You need to let Nate explain everything."

"No, please tell me." I look between him and Jess, begging for them to be honest with me.

"All he said is some girl he used to mess around with called him all scared and upset saying that her boyfriend had threatened to kill her. Nate tried to help and got her out of town, but the fucking guy is a psycho and tried to kill him."

"Fuck. Now it all makes sense," I whisper, and Jess hears me.

"What does?" she asks.

"I…" I'm in a cloud and have to pull myself out of it in order to speak. "I saw him today at the airport with her. I thought he was back with her."

Nash laughs out loud, "Are you serious?"

I look at him, waiting for a response, but he just stares at me slack-jawed. "Of course I'm serious. They kissed. What was I supposed to think?"

"I can guarantee he didn't kiss her."

"I saw it, Nash."

"Elania, you saw what you wanted to see. He was just trying to help her. Remember, she's crazy. He felt bad that she was in that situation. He blamed himself."

I'm silent, unsure of what to say next.

"El, he fucking loves you. I've known him for a long time, and trust me when I say, I've never seen him the way he has been since meeting you."

He loves me? My heart wrenches for him. I

need to see him and talk to him about everything. "Can I go back there?"

"He just went back for some tests, but should be out soon."

"Okay," I respond, following them back into the ER. As we walk through all of the hallways and doors, I imagine what Nate felt coming in here after being shot. I should have been there for him. I should have talked to him. Then maybe none of this would've happened.

"We're gonna run home and shower. If that's cool."

I nod my head, not able to look at them again with his blood all over them. I can't imagine Nate losing so much blood.

"Are you gonna be okay waiting for him?" Nash asks.

I nod my head and wave to them both watching me as they leave. Sitting on the edge of the window inside his room, I can still smell Nate in here. He's not far away and I thank God that he's alive.

I can't stop beating myself up for the way that I acted today. I should've talked things through with Nate. My fucking cheater-radar is on such a damn hair trigger, that I couldn't even bear to hear him out. But when the life of someone you love hangs in the balance, it puts a whole new perspective on things.

Leaning forward, I place my head in my hands while I wait. My mind drifts back to so many times with him. From the first time that I saw him in my office and had to pretend to be busy with the receptionist in order to compose myself, to the first time we had sex. Every second with him I've cherished. Minus the minor bumps, we've had a great relationship. Nate isn't perfect, but everyone can change...can't they?

"El?" the voice is raspy and I look up to see Nate being wheeled into the room.

I run to him practically throwing myself on top of him when the nurse stops the bed.

He holds me and we both begin to cry. I'd been so worried that I'd never get another chance with him. Today I thought it was the end for us, and now, here we are, reunited and he's alive. It's more than I can handle.

"How are you?" I ask, pulling back a little, our faces stay close to one another's while I wait for his response.

He blinks a few times and says, "I'm okay. I'm so sorry for today. I need to explain."

"I talked to Nash, and he told me some of what happened, but I still don't get why you don't tell me these things?"

"Listen, El, I fucked up. There's no denying that. I should have been honest with you."

"You should have. You can always tell me anything."

"That's just it. It's not you, El."

I look at him confused. "What do you mean?"

He clenches my hands even tighter. "It's me. I lie to protect myself." I stare at him a bit stunned, not sure how to respond. "El, I don't want to hide behind PTSD, and for the most part, I've learned to cope with how trauma has changed me. Then when stuff started to happen to me, when all of this started coming up, it was like telling you the truth wasn't an option."

"I don't know what you mean, Nate." There is a sense of pressure on my shoulders and I don't think I'm going to like his answer. Tears gloss over his eyes.

"It's part of what I went through when I was a POW and now being home. I guess I haven't quite handled everything. I think I put on a good front, but I do a lot of stupid shit to keep from feeling freaked out. Panicky and shit. God, I hate even saying this out loud."

I nod my head and lay my head down on his shoulder. I'm scared for what's next. How is he supposed to get over this? He places a hand on my head and in this moment, in this second, I promise to myself to never give up on Nate again. No matter what. I've known all along that he's damaged. I thought it was a lot like I am, but it's far worse than me.

I wake disoriented and out of it. I'm huddled in a ball and immediately reach for Nate, but he's out of my grasp. Blinking a few times, I try and pull the room together. Then it hits me. We're in the hospital.

I find Nate right away and focus on him, watching him sleep so peacefully. He's on his side, his face close to mine. Reaching up, I touch him, cupping his cheek before I get up and sneak out to the nurse's station where I can use a restroom.

The nurse smiles as I emerge, leaving the

door cracked. When I come back, I take the opportunity to ask the nurse what really happened to him.

"Mr. Wilcox lost a lot of blood after being shot in the shoulder. Thankfully the bullet didn't hit any nerves or bone and nothing serious was injured, so our surgeons were able to close the wound pretty easily, but he did lose a heck of a lot of blood."

"When can he go home?"

"In the next few days, as long as there are no complications."

I go back in and sit next to Nate, resting my head on the side of his bed while I trace my fingers gently over his arm. My stomach tightens as I think about the future. Tears fill my eyes and one droplet lands on his arm. Nate wraps his arm over my head holding me and asks, "What's the matter?"

"I'm worried, Nate."

"Why?" he asks.

"Because I don't know what the future has in store for us."

"No one knows what the future will bring them. But please, don't worry, baby, we'll figure it all out together."

As much as I want to believe his words, I can't. Nate hasn't been honest with me and that's unsettling, to say the least. Another tear drips on his arm.

"El, please tell me what I can do. I'll do anything to make things better."

"I don't know how to make me trust you," I say the words without looking at him. My heart is heavy as I fear the worst.

"We can go to counseling. Anything."

Lifting my head, I look him in the eyes. Christ, he's sexy. His hair is a mess and his dark eyes are so sad and filled with tears. "Please El, I'll do anything, but I can't lose you."

"I feel the same way. But the pain you've caused me and living with constant suspicion is not something that I want. It just isn't. Maybe we should take a break for a while, while you figure out why you can't be honest with me."

"No, El, dammit. I know why, it's the PTSD. I'll face it! I'm ready to! But please, please don't fucking leave me." His hands are wrapped so tightly around mine. But I have to pull away. I have to protect myself.

CHAPTER 34

-Nate-

Looking at myself in the mirror, I swear I've lost at least ten pounds. But working out right now is the last thing on my mind. All that consumes me is Elania and how I can make things right with her. Removing my bandage from where I got shot, the wound is almost healed. I decide to leave it off. The tape irritates the shit out of me, and today, I don't need any distractions.

Walking into my closet, I get dressed and take a moment as I do so to pray. I haven't prayed since I was a POW. But it helped me then, so I'm hoping it will do the same now.

Grabbing my car keys and phone, my stomach is a mess. I head to my car, regretting not eating today. But that's been a habit for me lately. It's 10:13am and I told El, I'd pick her up at 10:30. I make the quick trip to her place, all the while, I'm lost in my own thoughts. It's as if I'm in a trance.

I shake my head to clear the fog as I pull up to her house ten minutes early. Walking up, I don't know whether or not I should knock or go in. I realize then how ridiculous I'm being. Elania is mine. Yeah, we are going through some shit, but she hasn't completely left me, not yet. I need to be a man and face what's in front of me today if I want to hold on to her and what we have.

"Baby?" I call out walking inside.

"I'm upstairs," she yells down.

Her house smells amazing, the same way she does. My mind goes all over the place, thinking about how so recently I fucked her on this exact couch. Walking upstairs, she is doing her hair. I don't waste this opportunity and walk right up to her.

"You look gorgeous," I tell her wrapping my arms around her waist and looking at her reflection in the mirror.

"Thank you," she answers shyly.

"Did you sleep okay?" I ask, knowing she has been having a hard time without us staying together.

She shakes her head and I kiss her neck. She sets her flat iron down and watches my lips in the reflection. Grabbing a fistful of her hair, I move it out of the way, drenching her sweet skin with the love and adoration of my kisses.

She lets out a deep breath, exhaling heavily and I hold on to the hope that we will make it past all of this shit.

"Are you ready?" she asks, stopping my kisses from proceeding any further. I nod my head, a tad disappointed. But knowing that she only stopped me because she can't trust herself around me helps. That's why we aren't spending the nights together. She says if we do, then she will just give in and we will move past everything without handling what the real problems are. Normally, I'd push for nights together anyway. But I want a future with El and if I don't face my issues, it won't be possible.

Heading out, we get into my car and make the trip to Roger's office. He was very happy when I called and told him that we wanted to see him together. He said this is the first step towards me really facing my PTSD. He warned me, that more than likely, I wouldn't agree with what he had to say. But given that the current treatment he and I have done together seems to have failed me, I'm willing to hear his *plan,* whatever it might be.

Right now, I guess his *plan* is all I have to hold on to for my future. It's something that I am leaving up to him and El to decide. And believe me, giving that control away scares the motherfucking shit out of me. I've held on to all control since the moment I was found in Afghanistan. But for El, I'll do anything.

Neither of us says much and this is what scares me. When I am with her now, she's so much more closed. She's not the El that I used to know. She's different.

"Are you ready?" I ask her.

She nods her head looking at the tall building next to us.

I get out of the car as well, shaking away the anxiety before we head up. Roger's receptionist greets us with a smile and to my surprise, tells us to just go into his office. That never happens. But the door is half open. I knock once, holding El's hand tightly in mine. She smiles at me as we stand there and it gives me a sense that we will get through all of this.

Roger answers right away, "You can come in, Nathaniel."

Elania smirks at me and I know why. Roger

stands as we enter with a smile on his face.

"It's a pleasure to finally meet you, Elania," he says shaking her hand.

"Same to you," she responds.

"Please, have a seat," he directs us to his leather couch that I have spent so much time on. "How are you both holding up?" he asks.

We nod our heads and I sense that Elania is nervous. I saw Roger yesterday and filled him in about everything, so that a lot of the details didn't need to be rehashed in front of El.

"We're okay," I tell him. Her hand is still wrapped around mine.

"Elania, how are you?" he asks her point blank.

She shrugs her shoulders and shakes her head. I watch as a tear rolls down her cheek. He hands her a box of tissues and says, "I can see this is hard for you, especially with everything that has happened. But I want you to know that Nate cares very deeply for you, so I'm going to ask that you trust in me today, so we can begin to see if you and Nate can have a future together. I've been doing this a long time." She nods her head at him in agreement and my heart sinks. I just feel terrible for putting us in this situation.

"Now, Nate has agreed to do whatever we decide for him regarding treatment and that is an enormous sacrifice."

She looks at me and I rub away one of her tears.

"Elania, Nate told me what happened to bring you guys to this point. But I'd like to get your version?"

She recaps everything, even as hard as it is. Doing this gets her talking. It's not easy, I can clearly tell, but she loosens up to Roger.

"Then, last night I read online that PTSD sufferers often lie to protect themselves from ever getting hurt again. Do you think that's what Nate does?"

"Absolutely it's what he does. Would you agree, Nate?"

"Yeah," I admit, knowing how horrible it sounds.

"Why?" she asks so confused. "I mean, I could see him being controlling or something like that, because he lost his control, but he's not."

"Elania, PTSD affects people differently. For Nate, this is how it's affected him. Some people lash out in fits of rage. But for Nate, he just needs to protect himself at all costs. He often tries to put others first, to make himself think he's doing the right thing. But he's not helping himself."

"I want Nate to put himself first," she says looking right at me.

"I'm gonna try," I whisper.

"Good. Now I haven't told Nathaniel yet what my idea is, so please bear in mind that he might not like it. And Nathaniel, please remember that you've agreed to do whatever Elania and I recommend."

"And I will," I tell them. My stomach is a mess – giving my fate over to someone else is so hard.

"For a person with PTSD, to really move past it, they have to conquer their fears, often by reliving their past. Many times it can help to face what happened to them, so they can really put it behind them." I tense, already knowing what he is going to say. Elania places a second hand over mine. "There is a thirteen-week program at the local VA where veterans go and live to face what happened to them and to learn new coping skills. During this time, there is very limited contact with friends and family, and I'll be honest with you two, there is only about a forty percent graduation rate. But for those that complete the course, the transformation is night and day. I think this is what Nathaniel needs."

I fly up out of the seat and begin pacing the room. I can't be put away somewhere: away from my life, work, family, and El for over three months. "Talk to us," Roger says to me.

"I can't do that. Anything else, Roger, but being put away."

He laughs and it pisses me off. I stop and turn towards him. The anger burns so bad that I want to snap.

"Nate, no one is putting you away. You can leave at any time you choose. The completion of this program is solely up to you. I've been working with you for over a year and have done everything that I can for your PTSD. I think this is the best option for a jumpstart to get you to your ultimate goal of a healthy relationship with Elania."

I look at Elania. She's looking down at the ground, hurt by my reaction. She can't even bear to look at me. Causing her pain is the last thing in the world that I want. Another tear rolls down her cheek and lands on her pants.

As I watch the droplet spread into the fabric,

my decision is made. "I'll do it." For her I'll do anything.

She looks at me right away and I know that this is what I have to do. Even if it scares me to death. I have to do this. I cannot let her down. I love her and I'm not gonna risk losing her.

EPILOGUE

-Nate-
91 days later

"Leaving my life was…" I exhale holding on to the sides of the podium. My heart is pounding as I stare at the audience of people watching me. I use what I've learned in the program to calm my nerves. *God, how do I say it?* "It was one of the hardest things I've ever had to do. When you take the things in your life for granted, then are given a second chance, you can so easily slip into the same old habits. For me that's exactly what happened. I, like everyone else speaking here today, have my own story, but ultimately we all suffered through some sort of trauma during the war, resulting in our lives being forever changed." I look at my family and Elania, all sitting so proudly in the second row. "Today, I am up here because of my parents and my girlfriend." I point to them and El blows me a kiss. "I can look at them and all of you and say that I am thankfully leaving here a changed man. I've faced my demons and can now focus on the future and in doing so have the tools to not make the same mistakes again." I look at El as I speak those words letting her know that I've done this all for her and for us. "Thank you," I speak into the microphone before taking my place.

The crowd claps and it gives me a feeling of accomplishment. I was so nervous for the speech today. Hell, I've been nervous about it since I found out that I had to give it. But I did it because of the strength Elania gives me.

Listening to the last few guys give their speeches makes me realize just how damn lucky I am to have made it through the program. Not many of us did. I think over half of the vets left. But still, today there are thirteen of us. As the director gives the closing speech, I hold tightly to the journal that has been my outlet during this entire experience. From the day I walked in and left El and my parents, to reliving each and every torturous moment that I endured while I was held captive. Everything was written down in here, and I didn't do it for me, nor was it required by the facility. I did it for El. I want to be open and honest with her in every way imaginable. This journal does that.

The crowd disperses and everyone heads to the banquet room for our lunch gathering. I give both of my parents a hug. "I'm so proud of you," my mom says to me. Looking her in the eye, I say the same thing. She hugs me and I'm so grateful that I have both her and my dad here today as well. "Can I have a moment with El?" I ask them.

"Of course," my mom says, holding on to my shoulders.

I give her a kiss, then watch her walk off holding my dad's hand. I'm so proud of her and happy that she has come as far as she has. She is in great shape and has really kicked her MS in the ass, regaining much of her lost ground. She even moved back home, just like I will be doing today.

El stares up at me as gorgeous and loving as ever. Looking down at her, I really don't know how I got so fucking lucky, or why she even stuck by me. But, she did.

"I can't tell you how happy I am that this day is finally here," I tell her, holding her hand as we walk outside.

"I know, me too." I kiss her hand.

Walking outside, I head towards our favorite spot. Elania was able to come visit me every week for an hour on Sundays and we would always walk down the dock that spans out into the middle of the lake to just visit. Having this break was good in a sense. It was like we started our relationship over again.

But while I was away, it wasn't just about me. Elaina did a lot for herself too. After a short trip home to see her parents, she then started seeing Roger every week and she said that the visits with him have been tremendously helpful with the things she's been dealing with for a long time.

Both of us have come so far. We love each other and have known that for a long time now, and have built a solid foundation to rest that love on. "Nate, I'm so proud of you," she tells me as we reach the end of the pier.

"I'm just as proud of you, baby. You didn't give up on me and trusted in me, when I didn't make the best decisions."

"I love you, Nate, and I know you didn't mean for any of this to happen." She smiles as she speaks. "I know that you will never do anything to jeopardize us again."

"You're damn right I won't. El, I'm living every day going forward to make you happy. It's my number one goal."

She wraps her arms around me and I hold her back. The journal I am holding rests on the small of her back, practically burning me, I want to give it to her so badly. "I have something for you," I tell her, grasping it in one hand and pulling it around her body. She looks down at the tattered and worn dark grey leather notebook. Then she looks at me questioningly. "I want you to read this, if you'd like. Some of it is ugly on the days that I had to face my past. But it's me, my emotions, and the rawness of what I felt while we were apart. I want you to know everything about me. I'm not sure I can relive those experiences again, since I have put them behind me. But if you want to know about them, they are here for you."

She hesitantly takes the journal from my hands and clutches it to her chest. "I want to know everything about you, Nate. I'll always cherish this." Looking in to her eyes, I thread my fingers into her soft brown hair. She leans into my touch and moans a little. My cock twitches watching her. I need her so bad. I need her more than my body has ever needed anything.

Leaning down, I connect our lips. She grips my bicep and in this moment, I thank God for giving me a third chance at life. Not many can say that. But I can and will do things right this time. Her lips are so soft and loving, I have to stop kissing her 'cause I don't trust myself right now. I'm so horny for her, that if she touches me, I'm afraid I might fuck her right here.

"I love you, Elania," I tell her as she rests her head against my chest, still gripping the journal.

"Love you too, Nate."

I kiss her again and rest my forehead against hers. She looks at me with those dazzling eyes and says, "Let's go home."

ACKNOWLEDGEMENTS

As always, I have to first and foremost thank my husband. Without your support and love, I couldn't do this. You're my partner and your honest feedback truly makes these books what they are. You've made my dreams come true this year and for that, I am forever grateful. I love you more than you will ever know, babe.

To my remarkable editor, Lisa, this one's for you. You really brought this one home with the PTSD. Thank you for your patience with this book and then for getting it done under both of our time constraints. You are such an amazing and talented person and a great friend.

Leticia, as always you had my back. Thank you for pushing this baby to the top of your list; you are truly a miracle worker! I appreciate your help more than you know.

To my betas and street team, thank you. You all have stuck with me for so long. Each and every one of you has a special place in my heart. Your support, friendship, and honesty mean the world to me.

Last, but not least, to my fans and every single blogger that has stuck by me along the way. This series has only been possible because of you. You motivate me to be a better writer and to do what I do every day. I hope you've loved Nate's story and the conclusion to this series. If you could share your thoughts regarding the story with an Amazon review, I would be so grateful. Both the Prezident and I read each and every review that I receive.

Thank you again from the bottom of my heart. XOXO, LK